**"I want answers and I want them now,"
she said, her voice barely a whisper**

"Answers?" he calmly repeated. He inched closer, but stopped when Anna lifted the gun and aimed it right at his heart. "What do you mean?" She'd obviously figured out he wasn't the man she'd thought he was.

"Rafe and I were lovers," she whispered, a tear racing down her cheek.

"I'm sorry."

"Sorry?" she snapped. "It's a little too late for that, don't you think? Two months too late. I'm pregnant."

Oh, man. That knocked the breath right out of him. He couldn't speak. Couldn't move. All he could do was stand there and stare at her.

With her eyes brimming with tears, she levered the gun slightly higher. "And now I want to know what you've done with my baby's father."

Dear Harlequin Intrigue Reader,

Out like a lion! That's our Harlequin Intrigue lineup for March. As if you'd expect anything else.

Debra Webb concludes her trilogy THE SPECIALISTS with *Guardian of the Night*. Talk about sensuous and surreal and sexy. Man alive! You're sure to love this potent story that spans the night…and—to be sure—a lifetime. And you can find more COLBY AGENCY stories to follow this terrific spin-off later in the year.

Veteran Harlequin Intrigue author Patricia Rosemoor has created a new miniseries for you called CLUB UNDERCOVER. It's slick and secretive—just the way we like things here. *Fake I.D. Wife* is available this month and *VIP Protector* next month. So get your dancing shoes retreaded for this dynamic duo.

Finally we have two terrific theme promotions for you. *Claiming His Family* by Ann Voss Peterson is the newest addition to TOP SECRET BABIES. And *Marching Orders* by Delores Fossen kicks off MEN ON A MISSION. Who could ever resist a man in uniform?

So we hope you like our selections this month and we look forward to seeing you choose Harlequin Intrigue again for more great books of breathtaking romantic suspense.

Sincerely,

Denise O'Sullivan
Senior Editor
Harlequin Intrigue

MARCHING ORDERS

DELORES FOSSEN

HARLEQUIN®

TORONTO • NEW YORK • LONDON
AMSTERDAM • PARIS • SYDNEY • HAMBURG
STOCKHOLM • ATHENS • TOKYO • MILAN • MADRID
PRAGUE • WARSAW • BUDAPEST • AUCKLAND

ISBN 0-373-22704-3

MARCHING ORDERS

Copyright © 2003 by Delores Fossen

Visit us at www.eHarlequin.com

Printed in U.S.A.

ABOUT THE AUTHOR

Imagine a family tree that includes Texas cowboys, Choctaw and Cherokee Indians, a Louisiana pirate and a Scottish rebel who battled side by side with William Wallace. With ancestors like that, it's easy to understand why Texas author and former air force captain Delores Fossen feels as if she was genetically predisposed to writing romances. Along the way to fulfilling her DNA destiny, Delores married an air force Top Gun who just happens to be of Viking descent. With all those romantic bases covered, she doesn't have to look too far for inspiration.

Books by Delores Fossen

HARLEQUIN INTRIGUE
648—HIS CHILD
679—A MAN WORTH REMEMBERING
704—MARCHING ORDERS

Don't miss any of our special offers. Write to us at the following address for information on our newest releases.

Harlequin Reader Service
U.S.: 3010 Walden Ave., P.O. Box 1325, Buffalo, NY 14269
Canadian: P.O. Box 609, Fort Erie, Ont. L2A 5X3

Air Force Personnel Record

Name: Rafael "Rafe" M. McQuade

Rank: Captain (Officer-3 scale)

Classified

Career Field: Combat Rescue Officer

Security Clearance: Top Secret

Physical Description: Thick brown hair. Green eyes. Muscular 6' 1" body. No distinguishing marks.

Specialty Skills: Weapons expert, hand-to-hand combat specialist, proficient in three languages.

Duty Description: Commands combat rescue operations as a direct combatant, including survival, evasion, resistance and escape.

Current Assignment: Alpha Team Task Force

Availability Status: On medical leave, but called back for ultrasecret mission.

Diagnosis: Anterograde amnesia—may or may not recover previous memories.

CAST OF CHARACTERS

Captain Rafe McQuade—An air force Combat Rescue Officer who's kidnapped while on a special ops mission. His captors accidentally destroy key pieces of Rafe's memory—pieces that hold a deadly secret that puts Rafe, his bride and his unborn child in grave danger.

Anna Caldwell—She prays that Rafe can piece together the secrets buried in his memory in time to save them.

Colonel Ethan Shaw—Commander of the Alpha Team Task Force and Rafe's boss. Is he willing to let Anna and Rafe die to cover up a botched classified mission that could cost him his career?

Nicholas Sheldon—A security specialist who has a personal grudge against Colonel Shaw and Rafe. But has that grudge caused him to seek revenge?

Janine Billings—Anna's best friend who has ties to the very assassins who are trying to kill Rafe and Anna.

Special Agent Luke Buchanan—A Justice Department official assigned to the Alpha Team. The financial problems in his personal life might have caused him to betray Anna and Rafe.

To my editor, Priscilla Berthiaume.
Thanks so much for your guidance and support.

Prologue

A bullet slammed into the crumbling chimney just inches from Captain Rafe McQuade's head. He mumbled some vicious profanity and flattened his body against the battered roof of the abandoned hacienda.

"I've got an admirer," he snarled into the thumbnail-size communicator on the collar of his camouflage uniform. "Do me a favor, Rico, and take him out, will you?"

"I'm trying" was the reply he got from Captain Cal Rico.

All hell was breaking loose on the ground twenty feet below him. Artillery shells. Frantic shouts. The smell of battle, smoke and gunfire.

None of which was supposed to be happening.

Talk about Murphy's Law. Anything that could go wrong, had. And now his Alpha Team members—

and Anna—were neck-deep in cross fire between two warring rebel factions that had chosen this godforsaken place for a showdown.

Rafe inched forward, leaving the meager cover of the overhanging tree that he'd used to climb onto the building. His equipment belt and assault rifle scraped along the bleached roof tiles.

Come hell or high water, he would get Anna out. Failure was not an option.

"Infrared shows no one else inside the building. For now," Rico informed him through the receiver in Rafe's ear. "But Anna just moved into the cellar. You can access it through a door beneath the stairs."

"Atta girl," Rafe mumbled. With gunfire riddling the papery walls, the cellar was her best bet. Now, hopefully, she'd stay put until he got to her.

"I'm going in," he informed Rico.

Rafe scrambled to the lip of the roof, gripped onto the eaves and launched himself over the side. His feet crashed through the second-story window just below, and with his weapon ready to fire, he hit the floor running.

The hacienda had obviously been abandoned for months. Rafe fought his way through the litter of bashed furniture and debris to get to the stairs. He stopped at the landing and glanced down at the glass-strewn foyer. No sign of gunmen, but someone had shot out the windows and ripped off the double doors. The muggy breeze stirred what was left of a pair of ghostly white curtains. Just curtains.

Maybe.

Just outside the doorway, he saw a shadow of motion that had him holding his tongue.

Silently repositioning his weapon, Rafe waited. A second. Then two. Before he saw the man step into the foyer. A rebel fighter with an angry-looking machete and a semiautomatic. And he had his attention focused on the door that led to the cellar. Maybe the guy had actually seen Anna run in there. It didn't matter. There was no way Rafe would let him get to her.

No way.

The man looked up. A split-second glance as he tried to take aim. It was the last glance or aim he'd ever attempt. Rafe took him out with two shots to the head. The rebel fell into a heap on the floor.

"I just lost an admirer," Rafe reported to Rico.

Rafe barreled down the wide spiraling steps and made his way to the arch-shaped door beneath. "It's me—Rafe," he called out. "Open up, Anna!"

Almost immediately he heard her footsteps on the cellar stairs. With each one, his heart was right in his throat. There was a shuffle of movement before she opened the scarred door a fraction.

Rafe came face-to-face with a handgun.

Anna peered out at him, her gaze combing the foyer. Relief raced through him. And a whole host of other emotions that he didn't want to take the time to analyze.

"You came," she whispered, her voice shattering. She lowered her weapon. "I can't believe you came."

He pushed her back into the cellar and kicked the door shut, barricading it with the two-by-four and equipment bag already on the stairs. "Of course, I came. I'm an Air Force Combat Rescue Officer, darling. A highly trained CRO. Saving beautiful photographers is what I do best."

She made a soft sound of frightened laughter, slipped her firearm into her pocket and caught on to him.

Rafe was about to tell her how ticked off he was that she hadn't evacuated with the other journalists, but Anna stopped him. She latched her arms around him, and her mouth came to his. One kiss, and he forgot all about chewing her out.

Hell, he forgot how to breathe.

All Rafe knew was that he'd never, never wanted a kiss as much as he wanted that one.

Anna broke the mouth-to-mouth contact but held on tight. Rafe pushed the damp strands of honey-colored hair from her face and looked down at her. Her dark eyes shimmered with tears. Outside, the sounds of the fight began to fade, a clear indication that the Alpha Team was closing in.

"Anna's alive and well?" Rico asked into Rafe's earpiece.

Before he could answer, Rafe had to clear away the lump that'd settled in his throat. "Affirmative. Are we secure yet?"

"Only the area immediately surrounding the hacienda. Colonel Shaw's arranging transport for Anna, but you're looking at two hours, maybe three. I'll give you a rendezvous point and time when I have it. Hold your positions until further orders."

"Copy." Rafe clicked off the audio portion of his communicator. Two hours, maybe three. He could have waited weeks now that he knew Anna was all right.

"How did you find out I was here?" she asked, lifting her head from his shoulder.

"The Alpha Team's doing some jungle maneuvers so I've been keeping track of you since you arrived in Bogotá on assignment three days ago."

Anna gave him a considering look. "And with all the jungles in South America, you just happened to choose the remote village of Monte de Leon for those maneuvers?"

Rafe decided it was best to avoid answering that truthfully. "In a way."

A troubled sigh left her mouth, but she didn't ask for an explanation. Which was a good thing. He couldn't tell her about the classified mission that involved the Alpha Team, or the fact that he'd made sure he was close by in case something went wrong.

Rafe led her down the narrow steps and into the heart of the cellar. It was clammy, and the only light came from a bread-loaf size ventilation window at the back. He moved them as far away from that as he could, and with her snuggled in his arms, he sank onto a crumpled blanket in the corner.

"Soon we'll both be on our way back to Texas. Promise. Everything will be all right," he assured her.

Rafe leaned in and brushed his mouth over hers. It might have been just a brief kiss if she hadn't made a sound of relief, and pleasure. A throaty, feminine sound that sent a trickle of fire through his blood.

So, he kissed her, really kissed her, and deepened it when she responded.

Their bodies moved together, completing the intimate embrace. She wound her arms around him. Rafe did the same. Until they were plastered against each other.

Not good.

She latched on to his shoulders when he started to move away. "Is there any chance those rebels can get into this place?"

"Don't worry. We're safe."

Something he couldn't quite distinguish went through her eyes, and before he could figure out what, her mouth came to his again. Rafe felt the difference in her kiss. Not fear. Not this. This was all fire and need.

''Anna,'' he warned when she lay back onto the blanket. If he wanted to keep things in check, this probably shouldn't continue.

But it did.

Anna caught on to the front of his uniform and pulled him down with her. The logical part of his brain yelled that this would be hellish torture, but the rest of him didn't seem to care. While still holding on to his weapon, he buried his other hand in her hair and took her mouth as if it were his for the taking.

Rafe kissed her chin. Her neck. And the tender flesh that he found in the vee opening of her shirt. Anna arched against him, whispering his name.

When her leg brushed against the front of his pants, she stiffened slightly, obviously noticing that he was a dozen steps past basic foreplay. She didn't pull away, though. Not that he gave her much of a chance. Rafe knew this couldn't go where his body wanted it to go, but he wasn't ready to stop just yet.

While he kept up the assault on her neck, he opened the buttons on her shirt. One at a time. Slowly. As he bared her skin, he dropped kisses along the way until he reached her bra. It wasn't much of a barrier, a little swatch of pale-colored lace. He eased it down and took a moment to admire the view.

Thankfully, there was just enough light that he could see her. She was beautiful. And he didn't mean just her breasts and her body. Rafe stared down at her face and wondered what the hell he'd ever done to deserve her.

He lowered his head and brushed his tongue against one of her tightened nipples. She clamped on to her bottom lip, but not before she moaned with pleasure. He hadn't especially needed that kind of encouragement, but it sped up his plans a little. He drew her nipple into his mouth.

Anna's grip tightened around him. She arched her back and forced him closer. Rafe feasted. First one breast and then the other.

She stirred restlessly. Seeking. She pressed her lower body to his and had him seeing double when she moved against him in the most intimate kind of way that a woman could move against a man.

"I've been in this building for what seemed like an eternity," she whispered. "Thinking about you. About us. About how fragile life is. I want to be with you, Rafe, and I don't want to wait any longer."

He watched the words shape her lips. He'd already geared himself up to resist the need raging in his body. That's what he'd done for the past four and a half months since Anna had told him that she was a virgin and wouldn't give herself to a man she didn't love.

But those words changed everything.

He was about to remind her that it was the adrenaline talking, but Anna stopped him. She pressed her fingers to his mouth. ''I love you, Rafe, and I don't want you to say anything. I just want you to do something about it.''

His heart slammed against his chest. He had two simultaneous thoughts. *Thank goodness* and *oh, hell.*

Her timing couldn't have been worse. Ditto for the location. In fact, everything about the moment was wrong, wrong, wrong except for one major thing: somehow or another, it was right.

Totally, completely right.

Rafe let that sink in for a couple of moments. It sank in and went straight to his heart.

Maybe Anna didn't want the words now, but he sure as heck would say them to her later. Words to let her know that he didn't want to be just her first, or even her last, but her *only* lover.

He reached out, pulled her to him and took everything she offered.

Chapter One

San Antonio, Two Months Later

The moment Rafe slid his arm around her waist, Anna felt the jolt. Definitely not passion. Something else. Something she'd felt stirring just beneath the surface since his return three days earlier.

"No turning back now, darling," Rafe drawled, his voice low and intimate. The corner of his mouth hitched, causing a dimple to flash. "We've officially been joined at the hip."

"Yes," Anna managed to say.

She swallowed hard.

Rafe gently cupped her chin and leaned closer for the kiss that would seal the vows they had just taken. His hand trembled a little, and he closed the already narrow distance between them.

Their bodies came together. His crisp uniform whispered over the delicate layers of her silk-and-lace gown. Beneath her own trembling hand, Anna felt the strip of cool medals on his jacket and heard them jangle softly. All things considered, it was as perfect as it could be.

Except for that jolt.

Rafe kept the kiss brief, not much more than a touch. Breath met breath. His was warm and mint-scented. It mingled with the sweet fragrance of the pale peach roses in her bouquet.

''Don't worry,'' he murmured. The trace of Texas in his voice danced right off his words. ''We'll make up for lost time. Promise.''

It was the right thing to say. Ditto for the grin that curved his beautifully shaped mouth. But neither of those things made the jolt go away.

What in the name of heaven was wrong with her? She had it all. A mouth-watering husband that she loved. A life she wanted. This was her own personal version of a fairy tale come true. There was no reason for jolts or doubts.

None.

So, why didn't that make her feel better?

The chaplain placed a hand on each of their shoulders and turned them toward the guests. ''I'd like to present Captain and Mrs. Rafael McQuade.''

Applause rippled through the handful of people. Close friends and Rafe's co-workers, including his commanding officer, Colonel Ethan Shaw. The wedding had been so hastily thrown together that there hadn't been time to invite anyone from out of town. As unsteady as she felt, maybe that was a good thing.

When Rafe stepped away to speak to the guests, Anna saw her best friend, Janine, make a beeline right for her. Janine didn't waste any time. She draped an arm around Anna's shoulders and pulled her aside. "Okay, is this the part where you tell me what the heck's going on with you?"

Anna didn't stand a chance of denying that jolt. Not with Janine. So, she went for what would hopefully be a believable slant on the truth. "I guess my nerves are still a little raw. I just keep thinking that those rebels could have killed Rafe."

"Uh-huh." Janine gave her a flat look. "That sounds, uh, good, and it might even fool a few people. Not me, of course. Because you see, I'm not buying this I'm-worried-about-Rafe stuff. I was with you during those two months he was held captive in South America. I've seen the look you get when you're worried about him, and this isn't it, Anna."

Maybe not. But this wasn't the place to try to discuss something that might simply be a figment of her overactive imagination.

"Everything will be fine," Anna quickly assured her. With any luck, that was true. "By the way, thanks again for helping put this wedding together. I couldn't have done it without you."

Another flat look. "Does that mean if I keep asking what's wrong, you'll continue to make small talk?''

Anna nodded and put some grit in her voice. ''That's exactly what it means.''

''Okay.'' Janine shrugged. ''Then small talk it is. Mmm, let's see where we were.''

''I was thanking you for your help with the wedding.''

''Yes. And I was about to accept your thanks along with any future gifts of gratitude.'' Janine smiled, caught Anna's hand and lifted it so the light glimmered off the wedding band. ''A one-carat, emerald-cut diamond, nearly flawless. Rafe did good by you, huh?''

Anna stared at the ornate band. Since Janine owned a jewelry store and had perhaps helped Rafe pick it out, she wouldn't dare say that it wasn't her style. But it wasn't. Nowhere close.

Funny that Rafe hadn't known that.

She kissed Janine's cheek and got her moving toward the door. ''I'll meet you at the reception after the photographer's done.''

''More small talk?'' Janine questioned.

''Yep. Now, get going.''

Janine looked more than a little skeptical but thankfully didn't press the issue. She followed the rest of the guests when they began to trickle out to go to the Officers' Club at the base.

Anna stepped around the photographer, who was

making adjustments to his equipment. She knew him and offered a friendly smile. They often did freelance work for the same company.

Rafe sank onto the pew, folded his hands behind his head and stretched his legs out in front of him. There was nothing remotely odd about it. Anna had seen him do that a hundred times. Rafe didn't sit. He lounged. And it was that familiar pose that had her relaxing. It was *normal,* and if that was normal, then probably everything else was, too.

Probably.

As if he'd sensed that she was staring at him, Rafe looked up. "What? Having second thoughts already?" he asked, another grin shoving up the corner of his mouth.

She didn't have time to answer. There was a soft beep. Just one. It came from Colonel Shaw's pocket, and it was more than enough to get her complete attention.

The colonel pulled out the tiny phone and pressed it to his ear. "Alpha One," he said to the person on the other end of the line.

It seemed as if time ground to a screeching halt.

But only for a moment.

Something shattered. A loud deafening blast. Anna whirled toward the sound and saw the jagged multicolored pieces fly through the church. They'd come from the stained glass window behind the altar. Or rather, what was left of it. God, someone was shooting at them.

Just like that, Rafe sprang into action. He whipped out a sleek matte black gun from his shoulder harness and yelled for her to get down. Colonel Shaw did the same and hurried to turn off the lights.

The place was suddenly pitch-black, the darkness closing around her, and Anna found herself standing alone in the middle of a deadly silent room. She dropped to the floor, made her way to the organ and ducked behind it.

Lots of thoughts crossed her mind. None good. This was the culmination of all her nightmares. The rebels had come for Rafe, again, and this time he might not get so lucky.

She heard the footsteps. Barely. They were more movement of air than sound, but she didn't know what direction they were coming from. Not until the hand slid over her mouth.

"It's me," Rafe whispered. "Shhh."

He eased his hand from her mouth and moved her farther behind the organ. Without warning, he pushed her to the floor, a cloud of silk and lace fluffing up around her.

Anna held her breath and tried not to make a sound. Hard to stay quiet though when fear kept trying to grab her by the throat.

The moments crawled by. Slowly, her eyes adjusted to the darkness, and she peered out from behind the thick wooden base of the organ. Colonel Shaw was nowhere in sight. She prayed he hadn't gone outside, alone.

Of course, there weren't many alternatives.

Were there gunmen still out there? Maybe members of the rebel faction that had taken Rafe hostage? Or was this some other special ops mission? Maybe it didn't even matter. After all, a bullet could be deadly no matter what the motivation or cause behind it.

Only threads of moonlight filtered through the thick stained glass windows. It was too dark to see the photographer on the other side of the church, but she could hear him. His breath came out in short, fast spurts.

Unlike Rafe's.

Even though he loomed over her, only inches away, he was completely silent. If he had any reaction to the situation, he certainly didn't show it.

Something darted past one of the windows, casting a sinister shadow over the sanctuary. Rafe must have felt her body tense because he pressed his hand on her shoulder.

"Stay put," he warned in a rough whisper.

Anna latched on to his arm when he moved slightly. "You're not going out there, are you?"

"No. Colonel Shaw would want me to stay here with you. We have people all around the place. They can take care of the situation."

Anna hadn't known about the *people* who were outside guarding the church. But Rafe had. And so had his commanding officer. They obviously assumed something like this could happen, or they wouldn't have made such security arrangements.

What else did they know?

Another shadow slashed across the window, and a swish of sound followed. Maybe a gun rigged with a silencer and maybe just the wind rustling through the trees. But Anna didn't think it was the wind.

"At your six, Rafe," Colonel Shaw called out.

Rafe pivoted, took aim and fired twice. There was a spray of hot lead and glass. A sharp groan of pain.

And then the silence returned.

Anna counted off the seconds with each thud of her heartbeat. She wanted to ask Rafe if he was hurt, but she didn't dare risk it.

"The situation's contained," she heard a man announce. His voice hadn't come from inside the church, however, but out there somewhere on the other side of that shattered window.

The lights flared on, and in the same motion, Rafe sprang to his feet. Seemingly as an afterthought, he held out his hand and offered it to her so he could help her up from the floor.

"Are you okay?" he asked. Rafe reholstered his gun as calmly as he'd drawn it.

No. She wasn't. Along with the incident in Monte de Leon, these had been some of the most terrifying moments of her life. Anna gulped in a huge breath of air and glanced back at a gaping hole in the glass. She caught a glimpse of an Alpha Team member before he darted out of sight.

"What just happened?" she managed to ask.

"We'll know more when the colonel's had a chance to meet with the team." Rafe turned toward the photographer who was cowering near a pew. "Why don't you go ahead and pack up? We'll have pictures done some other time, okay?"

The man eagerly nodded and began to take down the equipment. Anna didn't intend to be placated quite so easily. "What's going on here, Rafe?"

He brushed a kiss on her cheek, took her by the hand and led her to a pew at the back of the church. "I'll go over everything with you after I've spoken to Colonel Shaw."

"In other words, there's something you don't want me to know." And by the time he did tell her, it most certainly wouldn't be *everything*. It would have been processed through layers and layers of debriefings until it was sanitized beyond recognition. "Who was out there?"

"Rafe?" Shaw again. "Come over here. I need a word with you."

Anna grabbed his arm. "I want to know what happened."

It seemed as if he was about to tell her, but then Shaw repeated the order he'd given just moments earlier. "It won't take long," the colonel added. This time, there was some impatience in his voice.

"We'll talk later," Rafe assured her. "And don't worry, everything will be fine."

"It'll be fine when you tell me—"

"Not now, Kate," he snapped. Rafe started to walk away but then came to a complete halt.

Kate.

He'd called her Kate, the name of Colonel Shaw's latest girlfriend.

Anna stared at him and felt her blood run cold.

Oh, my God. Who was this man she'd just married?

Who?

One thing was for certain, it wasn't Rafe Mc-Quade. Behind those familiar eyes and face, her husband was a stranger.

Chapter Two

Kate.

He'd called her Kate. Talk about a stupid mistake. It could jeopardize everything.

Rafe stared at her while he quickly tried to come up with an apology. Or at least a reasonable explanation. But she didn't look very receptive to whatever he had to say. There were a lot of questions in her eyes. And doubts. Doubts that he'd put there with that slip of the tongue.

How the devil could he have gotten her name wrong?

He lifted his hand to Colonel Shaw in a wait-a-minute gesture and went toward her. She stepped back. Not once. Twice. A clear signal that this wasn't a good time to try to pull her into his arms.

''Why?'' she asked, shaking her head. That wasn't the only thing shaking. Her bottom lip was none too steady.

"Because I made a mistake." It was a good start, but he was a long way from undoing the damage. "Because I was scared. The thought of losing you has a way of doing that to me. Believe me, I know who you are."

"Do you?" she demanded.

It wasn't anger he heard in her voice but fear. He would have preferred the anger.

"I know," he assured her. "You're Anna, the woman I love. The woman I married." He eased closer. Baby steps. And kept eye contact with her. Until he could finally reach out and touch her. He ran his fingers along her arm and rubbed gently. "And I'm so sorry."

Her breath settled a little. It wasn't an acceptance by a long shot, but it would have to do for now. Behind him, he could hear Colonel Shaw's impatient murmurings.

"I really need to do this debriefing," Rafe continued. "But when we're done, we'll talk. And if necessary I'll do some groveling, okay?" He threw in a grin, but it did nothing to soothe the tension on her face.

Rafe waited a moment to see if she had anything to say. She didn't. Anna only stared at him.

All right. So, this wasn't a five-minute fix. Not that he'd thought it would be. It was yet another contingency, a bad one, in a day already filled to the brim with contingencies.

"I won't be long." He gave her arm a gentle squeeze, turned and went to his boss.

"Problem?" Shaw asked the moment Rafe joined him on the other side of the church.

Rafe hesitated, debating how much he should tell, but from his boss's demeanor, he already had enough to deal with. "I can handle it. What's the situation with the shooter?"

"The guy's alive but not talking. No ID on him, but they might be able to get something when they run his prints."

It was a long shot, and they both knew it. "Any idea what he was doing out there?"

"He tried to tamper with the communication equipment. The team scoured the area and didn't find anyone else. Seems he was working alone."

Rafe had already figured that part out for himself, but it was good to hear his commanding officer verify it. If there had been others, they wouldn't be having this conversation, and his bride wouldn't be in the pew staring craters in him. The three of them would still be in the dark waiting for the remainder of Alpha Team to contain the situation.

He almost wished they were still waiting it out. Then, he'd have a second chance to take back what he said to Anna.

"I've got someone checking over the equipment to make sure everything is fine," Shaw said, his explanation low enough that Anna wouldn't be able to hear. "And it looks as if we'll have an all clear for you two to leave in a couple of minutes. I'll stay here to wrap up things."

Rafe made a sound of agreement and issued an obligatory thanks and farewell to the photographer when he hurried out the door. The guy looked scared out of his mind, and probably was. A definite case of the wrong place at the wrong time, but at least everyone was alive. It could have been much worse.

Much worse.

Shaw tipped his head to Anna and kept his voice to a whisper. "Is she all right?"

Rafe wanted to say yes, but he couldn't. Besides, with that stunned expression on her face, it was obvious that she was far from all right. "I called her by the wrong name."

"Hell," Shaw mumbled. "How did you explain that?"

"Slip of the tongue. The pressure of the situation. Imperfection." But it wasn't the explanation or excuses that mattered. "Sir, I'm not sure she believes me."

The colonel added another four-letter profanity. "I'll do some damage control," Shaw assured him, his voice a low, rough bark. "Anna trusts me."

It was true, but Rafe almost wished she didn't. If Shaw had been just another officer assigned to Alpha Team and hadn't been close friends with Anna's late father, then maybe the colonel would have come up with a different plan.

One that didn't involve a wedding by direct order.

"She'll find out, eventually," Rafe said more to himself than to Colonel Shaw. From all accounts Anna was a bright woman, and he was bound to make other slipups. Sooner or later, she'd catch on.

If she hadn't already.

Shaw looked him straight in the eye. "But she won't find out until this is over, understand? I won't have you jeopardize the lives of those men—or her—because your conscience is bothering you."

"It isn't my conscience that's giving me a problem, *sir*. It's the notion that we could have gone about this in a different way. We shouldn't have involved her in this."

"She's involved whether you want her to be or not," Shaw declared. "Besides, Anna wanted this marriage."

He could have argued that. He could have reminded the colonel that Anna Caldwell actually wanted to marry Captain Rafe McQuade. When Anna learned that he wasn't that man, she wouldn't be pleased. Worse, there was nothing he could do to stop it. Things had already been set into motion.

Hell, legally he was married to her.

"Just stick with the plan," Shaw continued. He motioned for a team member, Special Agent Luke Buchanan, to join them when he entered the church.

''We're too deep into this to back out now. Other than putting her under lock and key, this is the best way to keep her safe.''

Rafe was afraid that's what the colonel would say. It didn't make it easier to swallow. ''But what about the reception? We're expected there.'' In fact, it was more than expected. It was a vital part of the plan to generate some publicity.

Shaw blew out a long, frustrated breath. ''We'll postpone it. I don't want you out in the open, not after what just happened. I'll come up with an excuse why neither of you can be there.''

Rafe followed that through to its logical conclusion. If Anna and he didn't go to the reception, there would be no public appearance. No picture of the happy bride and groom in tomorrow's newspaper. No illusion to build a safety net for Anna and the others. And no diversion for him to make a much-needed exit.

Rafe repeated the four-letter word the colonel had just used.

Shaw checked his watch. ''The limo will take you and Anna to the VIP quarters at the base. I'll be here for the next few hours if you need to get in touch with me.''

VIP quarters. That wasn't the way things were supposed to work tonight. Shaw didn't give him a chance to remind him of that, but instead stepped away and headed toward Anna. Rafe watched as his boss took his bride's hand and urged her to her feet. Shaw leaned closer and whispered something that had her offering him a thin smile.

"It's apparently show time," Special Agent Buchanan mumbled when he walked closer to Rafe. "Again."

Yep. *Show time* was the right term for it. For the last three days, that was pretty much what all of them had done. It turned Rafe's stomach.

"By the way," Buchanan went on, "have I mentioned that I'll tear you limb from limb if you don't do everything in your power to stop Anna from getting hurt?"

"At least a hundred freaking times." But Rafe didn't hold the man's Neanderthal threat against him. Buchanan knew Anna and the other Alpha Team members. They weren't friends exactly, but this had to be taking a toll on him.

Too bad, though, that Rafe didn't see a way around this. He had to continue this charade, which would likely end with an innocent woman having her heart broken. It was the epitome of a rock and a hard place. And Anna was in the middle of it simply because she'd had the rotten luck to fall in love with the wrong guy.

He glanced over Buchanan's shoulder and saw the colonel and her making their way toward them. For a brief second, their gazes connected, but she quickly looked away. So, despite Shaw's confidence in his pseudo-fatherly relationship with Anna, he hadn't been able to smooth things over, after all.

"I was just telling Anna about that mud-for-brains idiot who thought it was a good idea to try to steal our equipment," Shaw announced. "Rafe winged the guy, but he'll be all right." The colonel passed the bouquet to her, and she gripped on to it as if it were a lifeline. "She's still a little shaken up. Heck, we all are. Right, Rafe?"

He mumbled a mandatory agreement and even tossed in one of his grins.

"How about it—are you sure you're okay?" Buchanan asked her.

Rafe didn't think it was his imagination that she gave Buchanan a suspicious glance, as well. With reason. Anna was probably trying to decide if she could trust any of them.

She finally nodded in response to Buchanan's question. "So, I guess you anticipated something like this might happen, or you wouldn't have had men outside the church?"

Rafe didn't even try to answer that. Thankfully, Colonel Shaw took the lead. "We didn't want to take any chances. Good thing, too, huh?"

"Yes. A good thing." But she didn't sound at all sure of the colonel's explanation.

Colonel Shaw put his arm around her shoulder. "Since you're probably not in a party mood, I thought it might be a good idea if we postpone the reception for a few days. Maybe you and Rafe could just go to the VIP quarters and leave for your honeymoon first thing in the morning? Don't worry. I'll let the guests know what's going on.''

She eased out of his grip. ''Was that man connected to the rebels who held Rafe hostage?''

''From all accounts, no, but we'll check him out. Don't worry. By tomorrow, we'll know everything about him, including his brand of toothpaste.'' Colonel Shaw looked at Buchanan and motioned toward the door. ''Why don't you and I make sure the limo's ready?''

Rafe mentally cursed. This was a ploy to get him alone with Anna. It was Shaw's way of telling him to finish the damage control he started.

''So we're staying at the base?'' Anna asked. Probably because the other two men walked away without answering her, she turned to him. ''Is that where we're spending our honeymoon?''

Forcing himself to move, he hooked his arm around her neck. ''Nope. That's a surprise, darling. We'll just stay the night there in case the local cops need to talk to me about the shooting.''

At least that was probably how the plan would work. They would have to wait in quarters until he got further orders from Shaw.

''Look, I'm really sorry about what happened,'' he told her. ''For the shooting and that stupid thing I said earlier. I'll do that groveling now if you like.''

He said it lightheartedly, but there was nothing humorous about the look that Anna gave him. However, it didn't last long. By degrees, her expression softened. Or something. A frustrated sigh left her mouth, and she stepped into his arms as if she belonged there.

"I'm scared," she confessed. "And I'm tired of feeling this way. I just want things to be normal again."

Rafe automatically tightened his grip around her. "I know."

"It was just such a shock when you called me Kate. I mean, you've never done anything like that before. I always think of you as, well, unshakeable." She buried her face against his neck. "I guess the pressure got to you."

"Oh, yes. It definitely got to me. I'll try very hard not to let it happen again."

But now what? He could go two directions with this. He could blow it off and try to make her laugh. Or he could confess that he was scared, too. Damn scared. He didn't have time for either.

Anna came up on her toes, with plans to kiss him no doubt. It certainly wouldn't be the first kiss they'd shared, but from all the signals she was giving, it wouldn't be chaste like the one at the altar.

He was right.

She wound her arm around his neck, her eyelashes fluttered down, and she fit her mouth to his.

It sure wasn't innocent. Nowhere near it. It was the kind of kiss a woman gave her new husband.

Hot. Needy. Raw.

Still, he didn't stop it. Nor did he pull away from her or do what he'd done for the past three days— make some stupid joke to break the tension. He just stood there and enjoyed a great kiss that he had no business enjoying.

She gripped the front of his jacket and pressed herself against him. Her breasts against his chest. It didn't matter if he *shouldn't* react, he did. But then his body didn't seem to understand that this was a game he had to play. A sick game with lives at stake.

He cursed himself. He had no right to kiss her this way. None. And yet he had no way to stop it. If Shaw's plan was to work, then Anna had to believe he was the man she'd fallen in love with months earlier.

She broke the kiss but kept her mouth close to his. So close that he could still taste her. "I want to make sure that we're okay," she whispered.

He didn't have to fake a laugh, even though this one was filled with frustration. "Oh, we're okay."

Well, with one exception—he was aroused beyond belief.

Not exactly the military bearing he'd hoped to maintain.

"You guys need a few more minutes or what?" he heard Buchanan call out.

Rafe broke away from her as if he'd just been caught doing something wrong. Which, in a way, he had.

Buchanan flexed an eyebrow, but other than that, there was no change in his neutral expression. ''Looks like you're ready to start the honeymoon. Come on. We'll get you to quarters as fast as we can.''

It hit Rafe then. With all the chaos of the shooting and the name incident, he'd forgotten one important detail.

This was his wedding night.

With the change in plans, it was also a night he could be expected to make love to his bride. There was just one problem with that. He couldn't. Because Anna didn't know the truth. And the truth was something he couldn't tell her.

Because if he did, it could end up costing Anna her life.

Chapter Three

Had she imagined that something was wrong? Had she imagined that jolt?

Maybe.

Anna stared at herself in the bathroom mirror and ran her fingertips over her mouth, remembering the way Rafe had kissed her at the chapel. That certainly seemed, well, normal. And incredible.

Maybe Colonel Shaw was right, and this was just a case of nerves. Wedding jitters combined with that horrible shooting incident. With all that had happened recently, a case of frayed nerves certainly seemed a reasonable response.

She shook her head, embarrassed at the way she'd behaved. Not only had she given Rafe the cold shoulder, she'd actually thought maybe he had been brainwashed. Or worse. It'd even crossed her mind that he was some sort of spy sent to infiltrate the Special Ops Unit at the base.

Talk about jumping to crazy conclusions.

Bolstered by her pep talk, Anna swiped on some transparent lip gloss, ran a hand through her hair and stepped back to give herself one last look in the mirror.

Well. The image she saw wouldn't have a G-rating, that's for sure.

The fire-engine-red nightgown covered all three of the important *S*'s required for a hot honeymoon night. Skimpy. Short. Sexy. Definitely meant to seduce. And that was exactly what she wanted to do. Then, after making wild, passionate love with her husband, maybe they could sit down and just talk. She had so many things to tell him.

"This is what I want," she reminded herself. "I love Rafe. I really love him." And she reached for the door.

The sound of his voice stopped her. Anna peered into the room and saw him on the bed with the phone pressed to his ear. His shoes and jacket were off, and he was in his usual lounging repose with his back against the headboard. He had his shirt unbuttoned, revealing a toned, tightly muscled chest sprinkled with dark brown coils of hair.

It was provocative. No doubt about it. Just the sight of him caused the heat to roar through her skimpily clad body. Mercy, she was one lucky woman.

He took a sip of water, set the glass next to his holster on the nightstand and spoke in soft, murmuring tones. She only caught a word here and there. *Security. Colonel Shaw.*

She started to join him, but something in his tone stopped her. It wasn't the tone of a man who simply wanted to clarify information. He sounded a little angry. Rafe fired off his terse responses in clips, like gunshots. *Yes. No way. We've been through that.*

Anna stepped back into the bathroom and put her ear against the door so she could listen to the rest of the conversation.

"It wasn't supposed to happen this way, sir," she heard Rafe say.

She felt the wave of doubt creeping up again, but she refused to let herself jump to conclusions. This probably had something to do with the cancellation of the reception. That's all. Or maybe something had gone wrong with his plans for their honeymoon.

Rafe continued. "I can't do that to her."

Anna froze. Held her breath. And waited.

"This won't work," Rafe snapped. "She's not stupid. If I stay here, she'll know. I think we need to come up with another plan."

Oh, God. What plan? Anna squeezed her eyes shut and frantically tried to come up with a reasonable explanation to all of this.

She couldn't.

No, she wasn't stupid, and she couldn't dismiss the gut feeling that something was wrong. Terribly wrong. Her instincts were screaming for her to listen, and she would. Finally.

So, now what? She could get dressed and try to sneak out of the suite without him noticing. The chances of that were slim to none, and even if she managed it, then what would she do? She could go to Janine's house, but that would just involve her friend in something potentially dangerous. Besides, it might be Rafe who was in danger.

Anna leaned against the wall. If Rafe was in some kind of trouble, she wanted to know about it. She might even be able to help, but first she had to know the truth.

She tried to steady herself by taking several deep breaths. One way or another she would have to convince him to tell her everything. And maybe it'd be a truth she could handle.

Before she could change her mind, she pulled open the door and stepped into the room.

His gaze snared her right away. "I have to go," he said into the phone, and then hung up.

He stared at her a moment—the hesitation all over his face—as he got to his feet. Well, maybe it wasn't hesitation. Anna rethought that theory when Rafe's eyes skimmed over her. From head to toe. It was a long, smoldering, appreciative look that stole her breath.

Forcing herself to say something, anything, she clutched the sides of her gown. "Do you like it?"

He made a sound, a soft rumble as if clearing his throat, and nodded.

"I'll take that as a yes." Anna stepped toward him, all the while wondering if this was the biggest, and last, mistake she would ever make.

WELL, HELL.

Now, how the heck was he supposed to handle this? And why hadn't Buchanan called? He was supposed to come up with some bogus plan to occupy him half the night. It was obvious from the way Anna was dressed that she had an entirely different idea about how to occupy him. An idea that would involve clothing removal and hot, sweaty sex.

"It's a yes," he assured his bride after he found his breath. "I definitely like the gown. Red, huh? It's a good color."

However, it was the woman inside it that he was really admiring. Rafe was glad he'd already loosened his collar, because just the sight of Anna would have required him to loosen something.

Damn. She was beautiful. Her dark-blond hair tumbled in a sexy heap onto her shoulders. Here was the sparkle he'd seen in the videos. Of course, he likely felt that way because of the barely there, devil-red nightgown that stopped at mid-thigh. High mid-thigh. If she bent just a little in any direction, he'd no doubt learn if her panties matched the color of the gown.

The blood rushed to his head. And other parts of him.

He couldn't let himself lose control. Nope. She might be his wife, but it was in name only. She certainly wasn't his for the taking.

Anna strolled toward him, her smile tentative. She was nervous. Rafe understood that feeling completely. He'd faced enemy fire and hadn't experienced the tangle of raw nerves that he felt right now.

He hitched a thumb toward a bottle of champagne. ''It's from Colonel Shaw.''

Rafe didn't intend to thank the man for it, either. Sometimes, he wondered if the colonel and he were on the same page. The last thing he needed tonight was to cloud his mind with alcohol.

Anna gave the champagne a passing glance. ''That was nice of him.''

Nibbling at her bottom lip, she stepped closer. And closer. Rafe just stood there while she lifted her hands and laced them around the back of his neck.

''I missed you so much when you were gone,'' she said softly. ''I mean, when we left each other in Monte de Leon, we thought we'd only be apart a couple of days. It turned into two long months.''

That comment ate away at him like nothing else could have. It was wrong to play with her emotions this way. Still, what choice did he have? He couldn't risk telling her everything. Not yet.

''I missed you, too,'' he answered.

Anna brushed her mouth over his. "But we're together now—just like you promised that day you put me on the transport to come back to the States. The day you asked me to marry you."

"I remember," Rafe lied.

She moved in for the kiss. He didn't quite manage to suppress a groan, but it didn't matter. Anna caught the sound with her mouth. She brought her sweet lips to his and gave him a kiss that nearly made him forget that this was supposed to be all for show.

She pulled back, slightly, and stared into his eyes. "I think we should start making up for lost time right now, don't you?"

But she didn't wait for him to answer that. She kissed him again.

Rafe braced himself for the assault. Or at least he tried to do that. It didn't work. Her taste slammed through his body. The energy. The intensity. And the distinctive feeling that he had lost his freaking mind. He had no business kissing her like this.

None.

Nada.

Zip.

He should be concentrating on a plausible lie to get him the heck out of there before he stripped that gown off her and hauled her in the general direction of the bed. Still, he didn't move. He stood there and took everything. The kiss. The heat of her body. Her.

Anna slipped her hand into his hair. "You don't

know how many times I wished that we hadn't agreed to wait until our wedding night to make love. Did you ever regret our decision to wait?'' she asked, her voice as silky as the gown she slid against his body.

Rafe couldn't look at her. Not even a glimpse. If he did, she would know something was wrong. Instead, he stared at her earring. A small pearl dangled on a delicate thread of gold.

''You better believe there were times I regretted it,'' he managed to say. ''In fact, the regrets went up a significant notch every time I laid eyes on you.''

He didn't have time to pray that she wouldn't question him further about it. Or time to come up with a lie that would give him an exit. He felt every muscle in her body go stiff.

Anna jerked away from him, and in the same motion she reached for his shoulder holster that he'd left on the nightstand. He could have stopped her from pulling the gun, easily, but it would have been a huge risk. If something had gone wrong, she might have gotten hurt. So, he just stood there while she drew his own weapon on him.

''Answers,'' she said, her voice barely a whisper. ''I want answers, and I want them now.''

He tried to play it light, but inside it was a whole different story. She'd obviously figured out he wasn't the man she thought he was. Now, the question was—what would she do about it? Would she really try to use that gun?

Maybe.

God knows what all of this would push her to do. If their positions were reversed, if he'd been kept in the dark about something like this, then he'd sure have that gun in his hand, and it'd be aimed at her.

"Answers?" he calmly repeated. He inched closer, but stopped when she lifted the gun and aimed it right at his heart. "What do you mean, darling?"

"The truth. There was no decision for us to wait," she clarified.

"Damn," he mumbled. Silently, he added some much harsher profanity.

He stared at her, cursing this stupid plan and cursing the fact that he hadn't stopped it. But there wasn't much he could do about that now.

Besides, he had a more urgent problem facing him. Literally. Somehow, he had to get the gun away from this woman without either of them getting hurt.

"Anna—"

But that's all he managed to say.

"Rafe and I were lovers," she whispered, a tear racing down her cheek.

There was no good comeback for that so he said the first thing that came to mind. "I'm sorry." He figured he'd be saying that plenty of times before the night was over.

"Sorry?" she snapped. Her eyes sliced at him with

a scalpel-sharp glare. ''It's a little late for that, don't you think? Two months too late. I'm pregnant.''

Oh, man. That knocked the breath right out of him. He couldn't speak. Couldn't move. All he could do was stand there and stare at her.

Pregnant!

Hell.

Anna was pregnant.

With her eyes brimming with tears, she levered the gun slightly higher. ''And now I want to know what you've done with my baby's father.''

Chapter Four

Anna's hands throbbed from the death grip she had on the gun. A dull ache drummed in her head, and her heart. What was left of her breath was lodged in her throat.

But those were the least of her worries.

Aches and throbs were nothing in the grand scheme of things. Not when her world had just spun completely out of control.

She tried to blink back the tears but failed. One slid down her cheek, and she feared others would follow.

"You're, uh…" He let out a ragged breath. "Pregnant?"

Anna nodded, not risking her voice. She hadn't meant to blurt it out like that. It'd been a secret, something wonderful and precious that she'd hoped to share with Rafe on their honeymoon. Instead, she'd shared it with this man.

This stranger.

He reached behind him, fumbled around until he located the bed, then sank down onto the mattress. He groaned and buried his face in his hand.

"Pregnant," he repeated. "Judas freaking priest! Why didn't somebody bother to tell me before now?"

His reaction confused her even more. He seemed far more concerned about her pregnancy than the fact she'd just discovered that he was an imposter.

"Who are you?" Anna asked.

He looked up at her and mumbled some words of frustration. "Why don't you put the gun down, and then we'll talk?"

"No." She had no intention of letting go of that gun. Not anytime soon. She already felt vulnerable enough standing there in the flimsy gown that she'd put on for what was supposed to be her wedding night.

Oh, God.

Her *wedding night.* And this man was supposed to be her husband. He wasn't. Anna was sure of that. But it suddenly didn't matter who he was. Because if he was there with her, then where was Rafe?

"Is Rafe dead?" She dreaded the question, but dreaded the answer even more.

He squeezed his eyes shut and groaned. "I knew this would happen. I just knew it."

That didn't do a thing to ease that ache. "Is he dead?" she repeated.

"No. Hell no."

She believed him. Or maybe she just wanted to believe him. It didn't matter. Anna latched on to that thread of hope. Rafe was alive, and as long as he was alive, somehow she would find him.

He opened his eyes, and his gaze snapped to hers. "I have to call someone. I'd rather you not shoot me when I try to do that. Deal?"

The almost arrogant request didn't sit well with her. Of course, at this point nothing would sit well except maybe to see the real Rafe come walking through the door.

"I'm not in a deal-making kind of mood." Anna raised the gun so he'd remember that she was the one in charge here. "Where's Rafe?"

He tapped his forehead. "Right here, darling. And before we start a game of twenty questions, Colonel Shaw needs to know about this, understand?"

So, Colonel Shaw was in on this—whatever *this* was. It made the cut even deeper since she'd known him since she was a child. It didn't help, either, that she was holding a gun on a man who was a dead ringer for someone that she loved more than life itself.

Ignoring her and the weapon, he snatched up the phone and punched in some numbers. Anna didn't have time to threaten him again, and from his resolute expression, it wouldn't have mattered. If this man was some spy, or some enemy combat specialist, then he likely knew that she couldn't pull the trigger.

Not with that too-familiar face staring at her.

It would be like shooting Rafe.

"We've got a huge problem," he said into the phone, then hung up. "Colonel Shaw will be here in a few minutes," he relayed to her.

"I don't want to wait for him. I want answers now. Why are you doing this? Who are you, and what have you done with Rafe?"

He began to button his shirt. What he didn't do was even spare her a glance. "That's a real long story. Best to put away that gun before you do something we'd both regret."

"I won't regret shooting you if you've harmed Rafe," she informed him.

He laughed, a short burst of sound, but there was no enjoyment in it. "God, you do love him, don't you?" He didn't wait for her to confirm it. "Believe me, I'm sorry about that. Sorry about the pregnancy, about everything. If I could have done this a different way, I would have. You deserve better than this."

Anna pushed his apology aside. "Where is he?"

She'd meant to make that question sound more like a demand, but her voice crumbled. More tears welled up in her eyes. It was hard to stay resolute when her heart was breaking into a thousand pieces.

"Please," Anna begged. "I need to know what's happened to him."

He lifted his hands in a why-me gesture. "I didn't lie about that." He tapped his forehead again. "He's here. *I'm* here. Things are just a little messed up right now."

She shook her head, not understanding. A whirlwind of emotions went through her. Fear. Doubt. Dread. Mostly dread. If this was Rafe, then obviously something terrible had happened. "Did they brainwash you?"

"Not exactly." He motioned toward the gun. "Look, why don't you put that down—"

"Not until you answer me, damn it!"

"All right." He stood and crammed his hands deep into his pockets. He didn't avoid looking her in the eye this time. "You want the story? Well, here it is. My captors used a so-called truth serum. A nasty barbiturate cocktail that did a real number on me and some of my brain cells. It had an unexpected side effect—retrograde memory loss—and the neurologist here at the base hasn't been able to reverse it."

She stared at him, afraid to feel relief that Rafe was alive, after all. "You have amnesia?"

He angled his head back and grimaced. "No. Well, not in the strictest sense of the word. Basically, I can remember everything except the last year of my life."

The last year. Twelve months. That didn't take long to sink in.

"We've known each other only a little more than a year," Anna mumbled.

He nodded.

And that brought her to the next logical conclusion. "You don't remember me?"

"No. Not really."

He didn't add anything to that for several long moments. Anna didn't dare try to speak. She just stood there, the gun gripped in her hand, and waited while her world fell apart.

"I remember meeting you right after I was stationed at Stennis Air Force Base," Rafe continued. "When I reported in to Colonel Shaw, you were in his office. You'd stopped by to tell him about a big assignment you'd just gotten."

Yes. She remembered. And that was several weeks prior to Rafe's and her first date.

Because she had no choice, Anna dropped down into the chair across from him. She fought hard to keep what little composure she had left. "Why didn't you tell me? Rafe, you married me, and you don't even know who I am."

He opened his mouth. Closed it. And shook his head. What he didn't do was offer anything else. No explanations. No assurances. Nothing.

There was a sharp knock on the door. The sound rifled through the silence and sent her stomach to her knees.

"That'll be Colonel Shaw," Rafe said. He glanced

at the door and then at the gun. "It's a good time to put that away."

He was right. The gun wouldn't solve any of this. Maybe nothing would. She was married to a man who didn't even know her.

Anna slowly released the grip she had on his pistol. Rafe eased it from her hand and placed it back in the holster on the nightstand.

There was another knock, but he ignored it. Standing over her, he reached out and brushed his knuckles over her cheek.

Anna flinched. "Don't," she insisted.

She had no idea what she should be feeling, but she knew for certain that she didn't want Rafe or anyone else to touch her. Too bad just looking at him caused her body to betray her. She had to battle the urge not to lean into his touch. To lean on him. Somehow, she had to convince her body that this wasn't the man her heart had fallen in love with.

He picked up his dark blue mess dress jacket from the foot of the bed and draped it around her shoulders. Only then did Anna remember that she had on just a nightgown. A nearly transparent one. She slipped her arms into the sleeves and hugged it to her so she was at least partly covered.

The jacket smelled like Rafe.

That too-familiar scent stirred an ache deep inside her and spelled out the hard reality of her situation.

The man she loved hadn't come home to her, after all.

Rafe answered the door, and she heard him whisper something to the colonel before Shaw entered. She didn't look at either of them. She couldn't. Anna kept her attention focused on the medals on the jacket.

"Pregnant?" Shaw whispered.

The barely audible conversation continued for several minutes, but Anna didn't even try to listen. She hated that the intimate details of her life were now part of some official discussion between two men she wasn't sure she could trust.

"I'm sorry, Anna," Shaw volunteered. "I didn't know about the baby. And I'd hoped things wouldn't have to come to this."

It wasn't the right thing to say. Her fear instantly turned to anger. "Did you think I was so stupid that I couldn't figure out something was wrong?"

"That's not what I meant." Shaw placed his hand on her shoulder. "We'd hoped that the blank spots in Rafe's memory would correct themselves by now."

"Blank spots," she repeated through slightly clenched teeth. The man was batting a thousand on the worst possible things to say. "I'm a blank spot, Colonel. And so is this baby I'm carrying. How the heck could you have let me go through with the wedding when you knew Rafe didn't remember me? I thought we were friends.''

''We are.'' Shaw stepped around the chair where she was seated and stood in front of her. ''Rafe was only following orders. *My* orders.''

Anna looked at Rafe, but he didn't verify that. In fact, he kept his expression blank just as he'd done in the church during the attack.

''I can't explain everything that you probably want to know,'' the colonel continued. ''But I can tell you that this is all part of a classified mission that involves other hostages—two CROs—who are being held by the same group of rebels who had Rafe.''

Her fingers stilled on the Purple Heart medal that she was fondling. ''What could our wedding possibly have to do with that?''

Rafe turned and faced her. ''I have information the rebel leader, Len Quivira, wants to make a swap for those two hostages.'' He paused, glanced at the colonel, and Shaw nodded. ''But there's a problem—I don't remember the information he wants. If he learns that, then he'll execute the men he's holding.''

Anna hadn't thought things could get worse, but he proved her wrong. She clutched the jacket against her heart. It was as if she'd awakened in the middle of a nightmare. God. People's lives were at stake just as Rafe's had been only days earlier.

Shaw took up the explanation where Rafe left off. ''The wedding had to go on as planned so we could make it seem as if everything was back to normal. The neurologist thinks Rafe's memory loss is temporary, that he should regain everything in the next couple of days.''

''And if it's not temporary?'' Anna asked.

Shaw never even hesitated. ''We're working out a contingency plan. But we need some time.''

Yes, and that's what her wedding had bought them. Time. Too bad it'd bought her much more than that. She was married to a man who didn't have a clue who she was. And she was pregnant with his child. A child he didn't even know he'd fathered. Heck, he hadn't remembered even making love to her.

She tried to bolster her expression before she looked at Rafe. A nearly impossible task. Everything about him—his face, his voice, his hands—everything reminded her that he was the man she loved. The man she wanted. And yet he wasn't that man at all.

''You could have told me all of this,'' she insisted. ''I would have gone through with the pretense of the wedding to protect those men.''

''We couldn't risk that,'' Shaw explained.

''But you could risk this?'' She gestured toward the champagne and the bed. ''Did you order Rafe to sleep with me as well?''

''No,'' the two men said in unison. It was Rafe who continued. ''Buchanan was going to come over here with some bogus emergency. He'd have stayed until morning.''

''Well, that would have taken care of ten hours or so. And then what, huh?''

Rafe shrugged. ''And then there would have been another fake emergency, and then another, until either my memory returned or until we managed to free the hostages. I wouldn't have slept with you.''

That confession didn't do a thing to ease the ache in her heart. ''Well, we'll never know, will we?'' she snapped.

Rafe met her gaze head on. ''*I* know.'' He turned away from her and strolled toward the window. ''I'm attracted to you. Maybe more than attracted, and I don't need a memory to tell me that. But I wouldn't have acted on that attraction without you knowing the truth.''

She swallowed hard. Even with the memory loss, he still felt the heat simmering between them. Heck, so did she. Anna cursed herself. Even now, she felt it. It was like a fire always smoldering inside her. That didn't mean, however, she would give in to it. After all, he'd lied to her about one of the most important things a person could lie about.

Colonel Shaw caught onto her hand. ''We wouldn't have done things this way if there weren't so much at stake.''

No, she didn't imagine he would. But she could guess where the rest of this conversation was leading.

"What do you want me to do—pretend I'm Mrs. Rafe McQuade?"

"For starters," the colonel said, "I need three days to put a plan into action. I can't negotiate with Quivira. That's against foreign policy. So, I'm stalling him, but he's suspicious because he knows what those truth drugs are capable of doing. Even if Rafe's memory returns, I probably can't trade that information for the hostages. In other words, I need a way to get my men out of there and put Quivira out of commission. All I'm asking is that you give me some time."

It was essentially an ultimatum. One she couldn't refuse. Either she continued this charade, or else she'd be responsible in part for those men's deaths.

Rafe was still at the window. He turned toward her and caught her gaze. The look that went through his eyes had her shivering. And aching.

Rather than speculate with a dozen different scenarios, none of which she'd probably like, Anna took the direct approach. "There's more?"

Rafe took a deep breath and strolled toward her. "We have an informant within the rebels' organization."

Anna shook her head. "Well, that doesn't sound like bad news—"

"The rebels plan to kidnap you," Rafe interrupted. "They want to use you for leverage to make sure I cooperate."

That nearly knocked the breath out of her. "Oh, God." Anna slid her hand protectively over her stomach. "When? How?"

"They won't get to you," Rafe assured her. "That's why we're here. I won't leave you unguarded until all of this is over."

It was too much for her to absorb. Anna blinked back the tears and cursed them. How had things gotten so twisted? A few hours ago, she was a happy bride. Now not only did her husband not remember her, they were all in danger. That included her baby.

"I know this is a shock, but here's what I need you to do," the colonel explained. "Tomorrow afternoon, Rafe and you will drive out to his aunt and uncle's cabin in the Hill Country near Canyon Lake. No one's using the place so you'll stay there until the situation with the hostages is contained."

She was already shaking her head before he finished. "What stops Quivira's men from finding out where we are and coming after us?"

"There'll be listening devices in the cabin. If anything goes wrong, all you have to do is yell, and we'll be there. We'll also have security specialists in the woods surrounding the cabin."

"That didn't do a lot of good at the church," she reminded him.

"Nothing like that will happen again."

Anna glanced at Rafe to see if he would second that. He didn't. He was staring out the window. His pose seemed almost calm, but she noticed that his hands were clenched. Not exactly the endorsement she'd hoped he could give her.

"So, all I'd have to do is stay at the cabin with Rafe for a couple of days?" Anna clarified.

Shaw nodded. "Only six people know about Rafe's lack of memory. Luke Buchanan. Communications specialist Nicholas Sheldon. The neurologist. And us."

"Luke is in on this." Anna shook her head. "I'm surprised he didn't say something."

"He couldn't," Shaw reminded her. "It has to stay that way, Anna. Tell no one else, including Janine."

"Janine? She's my best friend. Why couldn't—"

"No one," Rafe insisted. "We can't risk it."

His tone didn't leave much room for argument. "All right." But that was easier said than done. Janine had a way of ferreting out the truth. Anna would have to be careful when they talked.

"We'll have to convince everyone that we're really married," Rafe continued. "That means even the other security specialists who might end up standing guard in the woods won't know the truth. We have to make everyone believe that things are as they appear to be. If Quivira's men hear anything to make them think I've lost critical pieces of my memory, then the plan falls like a house of cards. That can't happen."

Anna drew in her breath. Whatever he was implying, she didn't think she would like it. That was nothing new. She hadn't cared much for any of this. "So, what are you saying?"

"Colonel Shaw needs time to get those men out so we can protect you. For that to happen, we'll have to pretend to be newlyweds."

She shook her head. "Yes, I got that. But how? In what way?"

Rafe turned and faced her. "*Every* way."

Anna pulled back her shoulders and waited for him to finish.

"The cabin has one bedroom. Just one," Rafe explained. "And we'll have to share it."

Chapter Five

With Anna right next to him, Rafe stood in the doorway and glanced around the living room of the rustic cabin.

''Man, talk about a blast from the past,'' he mumbled.

The place hadn't changed a bit. There was a massive bay window that provided a view of the lush Texas Hill Country. Battered hardwood floors dotted with colorful throw rugs. A well-worn leather sofa positioned right in front of a huge stone fireplace.

It was just as he remembered it.

Every strip of the golden pine paneling. Every picture on the wall. Every garage-sale knickknack on the mantel that Aunt Alice and Uncle Pete had placed there over the years. Rafe remembered it all.

Too bad he couldn't say the same for everything else in his life.

Especially his wife.

Not exactly the sort of thing a newly married man

should have trouble recalling. But other than their first meeting in Shaw's office and the information he'd accumulated about Anna over the last four days, he knew practically nothing about the woman beside him. The woman he'd promised to love, honor and cherish for the rest of his life.

Ditto for that part about making a baby with her. That definitely was a piece of this freaking memory puzzle that he needed to recall in a hurry.

A baby!

How he could possibly not remember making a baby?

Anna stepped inside with him, her attention focused on the cabin where they would stay the next seventy-two hours. Together. Pretending they were newlyweds.

No pressure, right?

"We'll have the place to ourselves," he offered, forcing himself to say something. He put his duffel bag in the hall closet. "My aunt and uncle are in their RV headed off to the Grand Canyon."

And if his present situation hadn't been so uncertain, he would have called and asked them to come back for the wedding. In just about every way that counted, they were his parents. Rafe had never even met his own father, and he hadn't seen his mother since he was sixteen when she left their hometown of Crystal Creek, Texas, to *find herself.* Presumably, she was still looking since she'd been at it thirteen years and hadn't bothered to return.

"The kitchen's that way," Rafe said, giving her the nickel tour. He pointed to the pass-through on the other side of the room. "Colonel Shaw supposedly had the fridge stocked."

Anna made a sound of approval, but Rafe saw no such approval in her eyes. As she'd done since they left the base, she'd confined her answers to just a couple of words or those approving-disapproving sounds.

"It's all right for us to talk," he said. "Sheldon hasn't turned on the equipment yet. And if he has to switch off shifts with someone, he'll give us a heads-up so we won't say anything we shouldn't."

Another nod.

All right. He obviously wasn't making a lot of progress in the area of mending fences. Much more of this, and he'd have to start groveling.

"The bathroom and bedroom are down the hall," Rafe continued. "Just one bed. Sorry. I can sleep on the floor, but we have to stay in the same room in case something goes wrong and I have to get you out of here."

Anna gave him a look that could have frozen molten lava, then started to walk away.

He caught her arm to stop her, but Anna glanced at the grip he had on her arm and slowly lifted her eyes.

"Look, I'm not jumping for joy about these arrangements, either," Rafe informed her. "But there's not a lot we can do about it. Quivira and his men mean business. Trust me, you don't want them to get their hands on you."

The iciness in her eyes thawed a degree or two, but she still dropped back a step, putting some distance between them.

"I know what we have to do," she snapped. "Believe me, I don't want to be kidnapped, but this is all just so…well, it's so…" Anna obviously gave up trying to get that particular point across and groaned. "Do you have any idea how hard it is for me to be here with you like this?"

Rafe nodded. "Yeah. I've given it some thought."

It had to be her own personal version of hell. By her own admission, she was in love with the man he used to be. But it damn sure wasn't a bed of roses for him, either. He was looking at a woman, a stranger, who happened to have his child inside her.

She made a helpless gesture with her hands. "It hurts to look at your face, to know that things might never be the way they used to be."

That touched him in a way that nothing else could have. Rafe reached for her, but she pushed him away.

"That won't help," she insisted.

He didn't press her, but Rafe wanted nothing more than to reassure her. Too bad that was the very thing he couldn't do. There were no reassurances. Until his memory returned or until those men were free, he was essentially in purgatory and Anna was doing penance right along with him.

"I need a couple of minutes to myself," she insisted. She pulled her phone from the purse she had hooked over her shoulder. "I'll call Janine and let her know that we arrived safely."

Rafe had to stop her again. "You can't use your phone. Sorry. It's not a secure line. You can use the one in the bedroom. It's cordless so you can take it anywhere in the cabin that you want."

"Can I give Janine the number, or is that not allowed?"

"It's allowed. The phone can't be traced to a specific location."

She mumbled a thanks, which had a get-away-from-me tone to it, and headed down the hall.

Rafe just stood there and stared at the empty space. Maybe it was time for that groveling. Either that, or the next three days would be even harder than he'd imagined, and he'd imagined a pretty tough time.

"A baby," he mumbled under his breath. He scrubbed his hands over his face. "A baby."

A child was the ultimate complication. And yet in some ways, it didn't feel so much like a complication at all. The baby was his. *His* baby. There was no doubt about that in his mind. Anna wasn't the sort to leave him and climb into bed with another man.

So, no matter what happened, the fact wouldn't

change that she was pregnant. It created a bond between Anna and him, whether she wanted that bond or not.

Too bad that bond could also create a distraction that he didn't need right now.

For safety's sake, he had to put aside his impending fatherhood and press on with the plan.

Hopefully, he could do that.

Rafe started to check on Anna, but he heard Nicholas Sheldon's voice in the tiny earpiece that he was wearing. "Rafe, I connected a couple of minutes ago. I can hear you loud and clear."

Great. Just freaking great. That meant Sheldon had listened in on the very private conversation he'd just had with Anna. Sheldon wasn't supposed to turn on the equipment until Rafe gave him the go-ahead.

"I've got a good audio and visual of all rooms except the bathroom," Sheldon continued. "We opted to stay out of there for your bride's sake."

"I'm sure she'll appreciate that," Rafe grumbled.

"We aim to please, Cap'n," Sheldon countered. "I can pick up anything louder than a whisper. And just for the record—I don't plan to play Peeping Tom or Eavesdropping Eddie while I'm out here."

No, but Sheldon wouldn't have much of a choice. He had to monitor the place. If the rebels found out where they were staying, they'd likely try to come after Anna.

"I'm in a bunker in the bluff that's visible from

the living room window,'' Sheldon went on. "It's a glorified hole, but I'll be monitoring the equipment from here. And I'm armed with some pretty nifty high-powered rebel stoppers in case something goes wrong. There's also a team at the bottom of the road to make sure no one gets through. That should give you a little peace of mind.''

Rafe glanced out the window at the bluff where Sheldon had indicated. "You picked a good spot.''

There were dozens of crevices in the side of that steep limestone bluff, and the bunker blended right in. But Sheldon was wrong about one thing. It didn't give him any peace of mind. Not much would at this point.

"Colonel Shaw asked me to pass on an update about that shadow you shot at the church. He didn't pull through.''

"Damn,'' Rafe mumbled.

"Yep. That's what the colonel said, too, along with some other creative profanity that blistered our ears. The guy was connected to Len Quivira and his rebels. No doubt about it. That means Quivira hasn't given up on his quest to kidnap Anna.''

And he wouldn't give up. Rafe didn't have a lot of memories about his captivity, but he'd seen the look of absolute determination in the rebel leader's eyes right before the Alpha Team stormed the encampment and rescued him. Quivira managed to escape, but several of his men were killed that night.

No, Quivira wouldn't give up.

But then, neither would he.

"Just give a yell if you need me," Sheldon instructed. "I'll keep you and your bride as safe as I can. Until then—adios, Cap'n."

Rafe wished that assurance had come from his best friend, Cal Rico. But Rico was still undercover down in South America. Sheldon was the newest member of the team, and a civilian at that. A contracted communications specialist hired by the Department of Defense. Still, Sheldon seemed to have all the qualifications necessary to make this a successful mission. And if not, then Rafe didn't intend to stand around and let Quivira and his rebels take Anna.

Nope.

He ran his hand over the gun in his shoulder harness. This time he was on his own turf, not trapped in the jungle, and he was ready for them.

"Did I hear you talking to someone?" Anna asked.

Rafe looked up and saw her standing in the bedroom doorway. He didn't think it was his imagination that she looked pale.

He tapped his ear. "Nicholas Sheldon was just testing out the equipment. How's Janine?"

"Talkative. Don't worry—I didn't mention a word about your memory loss." She laid her purse on the dresser next to the door. "Am I allowed to ask how much privacy I'll have while I'm here?"

"Virtually none unless you whisper or go into the bathroom. Sheldon is monitoring everything. And those tiny black things on the ceilings?" Rafe pointed to the one just overhead. "Not spiders. Cameras."

She mumbled something under her breath. "You know, I wouldn't mind if I thought for sure it'd keep us safe."

"I'll do my best."

"Let's hope that's enough." She didn't even spare him a glance and walked right past him.

The hall was narrow, and when she moved, she brushed against him. Her hip against his. Not good. His body reacted not just to the brief contact but also to Anna. Cursing himself, Rafe pushed aside that reaction. He didn't have time for those kinds of reactions.

He followed her into the living room, dropped down onto the sofa and tried to get his mind on something else other than the too obvious heat that crackled between them. "If it'll help, you can go ahead and yell at me for not telling you the truth sooner."

Anna picked up a picture from the mantel, studied it and put it back down. "It wouldn't help."

"You sure about that? A good surge of adrenaline might get you past the I-think-you're-fungus stage."

If she had a reaction to his attempted humor, she didn't show it. "I've had all the adrenaline surges I need, thank you. My trip to Monte de Leon and that shooting incident at the church were enough to last me a lifetime.''

"I know what you mean." He tucked his hands behind his head and sank deeper into the sofa. "And speaking of that incident, the guy didn't pull through."

She'd already started to reach for another picture, but her hand stopped. "Was he, uh, one of them?"

"Yeah. He belonged to Quivira's group."

She caught on to the mantel and closed her eyes.

Because she looked ready to faint, Rafe bolted from the sofa and hurried to her. "Are you all right?"

"Just a little light-headed. It might be routine for you, but I guess I'm just not accustomed to hearing about people dying."

"Believe me, it's not routine for me, either."

She stepped away from him when he reached for her. This time, Rafe didn't let her get away with that little evasive maneuver. He slipped his arm around her waist and held on. "When's the last time you had something to eat?"

"Uh, this morning at breakfast."

"Nearly six hours ago, and if I recall, all you had was toast and juice. No wonder you're light-headed. Come on, let's see what we can find in the kitchen."

He led her to the kitchen bar counter and eased her onto the stool. The silence suddenly seemed deaf-

ening. It was strange. They had so much to talk
about, and yet even more that he wanted to avoid.
For now, the baby had to be off-limits. It was too
much like a walloping punch in the solar plexus to
think about it. Still, it seemed with all that had happened, she would have something to say to him.

''Why are looking at me like that?'' she asked.

Only then did he realize he'd been staring at her.

''I was just thinking—about a lot of things. You
never did tell me how you figured out that I didn't
know who you were.'' It seemed a good time to turn
away and do something that didn't involve staring.
He rummaged through the fridge and came up with
some sodas and turkey sandwiches. ''What gave me
away?''

She kept her attention focused on the food he put
in front of her. ''The kiss at the altar.''

''Wow. The kiss?'' He shook his head. ''That
stings a little. And here I thought there wasn't anything wrong with that.'' In fact, for him it'd been
downright memorable. But then, he could say that
about every kiss he'd had with Anna so far. ''So,
why did that make you suspicious?''

She pulled off a tiny piece of the bread and put it
in her mouth. ''Your hand trembled when you
kissed me.''

''A tremble gave me away? Jeez Louise.'' He darn
sure hadn't noticed that. ''Makes sense, though, I
guess. Rico is always saying when it comes to tense

situations, I'm as calm as a virgin taking a home-pregnancy test.''

Anna sputtered out a cough.

The minute the words left his mouth, Rafe knew he'd made yet another mistake. For the next couple of days, he needed to strike the word *pregnancy* from his vocabulary.

''Say, are you all right?'' Rafe asked.

She waved him off and downed a couple of sips of soda. ''I'm fine. The bread just went down the wrong way.'' She paused. ''Your friend's right—you're not the trembling kind.''

Rafe stayed on his side of the counter, and while he took a bite of his sandwich, he gave that some thought. A tremble. Who would have thought something so simple would have blown the original plan? ''Guess I was nervous standing there at the altar,'' he said almost idly.

''You're not the nervous kind, either,'' Anna informed him.

He nearly laughed. Man, she was *so* wrong. He had no idea how many nerves there were in the human body, but he felt every one of them. The woman certainly had an effect on him. Maybe it was a good idea to strike thoughts like *need* and *want* from his mental vocabulary, as well.

Rafe downed some of his soda. ''I thought you figured me out because I hadn't remembered that we'd made love.''

"That only confirmed it."

It was a subject he should leave well enough alone, but Rafe couldn't. It was something that had been niggling at him since she discovered the truth. "A couple of days ago, I read an old e-mail that you sent to me the morning you left on assignment to South America. You talked about…well, about us—"

"Making love." Anna moistened her lips. "Or rather *not* making love. I'd told you that I intended to wait…well, for whatever, but I changed my mind that afternoon in Monte de Leon."

Oh. So, they'd made love just that once. Well, maybe twice. He glanced at her. Yep. Definitely—at least twice.

Rafe tried hard to recall any little piece of that afternoon, but that particular pool of memories was blank. Too bad. He was sure it was an experience worth remembering. Plus, it seemed only right that he should remember the occasion where they'd created a baby.

"I might be twenty-five, but I have old-fashioned ideas about sex, I guess," Anna continued. She kept her voice at a whisper, probably so that Sheldon wouldn't hear her. "Catholic guilt coupled with crate-size personal baggage. My mother slept around a lot, and I saw how much that hurt my father." She cleared her throat. "It hurt me, too. The gossip. The endless stream of lovers that she brought to the house while he was at work."

He slid his hand over hers. "I'm sorry."

She grimaced. "I have no idea why I just told you that. It doesn't matter. It was a long time ago."

Rafe listened to the nuance of each word and didn't care much for his interpretation. "Did one of your mother's lovers try to touch you or something?" He whispered as well. Even though Sheldon had said he wouldn't eavesdrop, this was one part of the conversation Rafe intended to keep private.

Surprise sprinted through her eyes. "No. God, no. Nothing like that."

His stomach landed somewhere in the vicinity of his boots. "You were a virgin?"

Her silence, and the way her face bleached out said it all. Damn it. A virgin.

She pushed the sandwich aside, eased her hand from his and stood. "If you don't mind, I think I'll lie down for a while. I didn't sleep much last night, and I can hardly keep my eyes open."

He couldn't let her just leave again. Not without one more attempt to mend this vast bridge between them. "You do know I would have come up with a different plan if I could have?"

Anna didn't answer him right away. "I know. You might not remember me, but I don't think you'd do anything intentionally cruel. After all, buried beneath all those blank spots, you're still Rafe."

Yes, he was.

And that brought him back to something that had

been on his mind since he'd stood at that altar—and trembled. This was a woman he'd already fallen in love with once. If things were different, if they hadn't been tossed into an impossible situation, it might even have happened again.

Might.

Unfortunately, he had a couple of strikes against him. He'd lied to her. Not a little lie, either. A bona fide whopper. Added to that was the fact he'd taken her virginity, gotten her pregnant and couldn't even remember doing it. And one more clincher—Anna no longer trusted him.

Not exactly a great recipe for building a loving relationship.

So, even if he fully recovered his memory, there was an ice cube's chance in a blazing furnace that she'd ever love him again the way she used to love him. He'd blown what was probably the best thing that ever happened to him.

"I should have said this before now," he whispered. "But thank you for everything. For the ceremony. For your cooperation. For this."

Anna just stood there, only inches away, her sweet feminine scent stirring around him. Rafe took in that scent. Cataloged it. Savored it. And forced away the ache that it awakened inside him. He prayed it'd give the blank spots in his memory a much-needed nudge.

It didn't. It only made that ache worse.

And it aroused him.

Before Rafe could do something stupid and act on that ache, Anna thankfully turned and walked to the bedroom. He waited several moments until he heard the springs groan on the old bed. Then he grabbed a beer from the fridge and went to the doorway to stand guard.

Since she was on her side with her back to him, Rafe looked at her. Like her scent, he cataloged and savored her curved body on the patchwork quilt. Her golden hair against the white pillow. Her creamy, pale skin.

She was an attractive woman. No doubt about it. But she was more than that. For lack of a better word, Anna was special. And to think, she'd given herself to him.

Only him.

Rafe twisted off the beer cap and brought the bottle to his mouth for a long, much-needed drink. His hand didn't tremble. Not this time. But deep inside him—well, that was a whole different story.

Anna and he hadn't just made love in that cellar in Monte de Leon. They'd made a baby as well.

His baby.

Rafe wondered just how long it would take him to absorb the enormity of that.

His baby!

Fury suddenly raged through him. Part of him wanted to take hold of every person who'd fired shots at Anna and beat them to a bloody pulp. How dare those SOBs risk Anna's life and the life of their unborn child.

However, another part of him wanted to surrender to the enormity of it all. It was humbling, and terrifying, like a mega jolt of reality. In seven months, give or take a few days, he'd become a father.

But first, he had to keep both Anna and the baby alive.

Chapter Six

"You didn't tell Rafe about the impending pitter-patter of little feet, did you?" Janine asked. Her skepticism came through even with Rafe's shower droning in the background.

As Anna had done with the rest of the telephone conversation, she chose her words carefully. Rafe had assured her that Colonel Shaw hadn't planted listening devices in the bathroom, but she didn't want to risk Sheldon or Rafe overhearing this particular part of her discussion. And she didn't dare move out into the hallway with the cordless phone because Rafe had insisted that he didn't want her out of his sight.

"I told him," she whispered to Janine.

"And? Don't make me beg here, Anna. How did he take the news?"

It was a good question, but Anna didn't know the answer. Rafe had said as little as possible about the baby. It was almost as if he'd been able to put something that monumental out of his mind.

Unlike her.

It was there. Always there. She worried both for her baby's safety and future.

"Rafe's very happy about it," Anna lied.

Janine's silence wasn't good. Anna could almost hear the wheels turning in her friend's head, so she went on the offensive. "We've been busy so we haven't had much of a chance to pick out names or anything. But there's plenty of time for that later."

Anna made sure she added enough inflection on the word *busy,* that it implied something of a sexual nature.

That wasn't a complete lie.

There was certainly a lot of intensity crackling between Rafe and her. Well, she felt the crackle and the intensity, anyway. That probably had something to do with the fact she was sitting on the bathroom floor only a couple of feet away from where he was showering.

The vinyl curtain didn't help, either. It was opaque and well worn in spots. The overhead light filtered right through the curtain so she could see in perfect detail the outline of Rafe's naked body.

Mercy, the man was built.

When he'd first informed her that he needed a shower, and that she'd be present for it, Anna figured out right away that it wouldn't be a comfortable ar-

rangement. A huge understatement. Rafe had un-
dressed behind the shower curtain. Thankfully. But
Anna had been fully aware of each article of clothing
that he discarded on the floor.

His white T-shirt.

Then, his snug jeans.

And finally, his steel-blue boxers.

By the time he was done, her pulse was hammer-
ing out of control.

"I won't be able to talk much longer," Anna continued. Best to say as little as possible to Janine to
reduce her chances of slipping up. "Rafe's almost
done with his shower. By the way, you haven't said
exactly why you called."

"Well, it wasn't just to interrupt your honeymoon.
I dropped by your apartment to water your plants and
check your messages. Your obstetrician had called."

Anna went stiff. "What'd he want?"

"Nothing's wrong," Janine assured her. "He just
said you needed to take some iron pills along with
your prenatal vitamins. He called in a prescription
and wants you to pick it up when you get back."

"You're sure that's all?"

"Absolutely." Janine paused. "I'm worried about
you, though, you know. You just don't sound like a
woman who's on her honeymoon."

"That's because I'm on the phone with you,"
Anna teased. "Would you feel better if I were
breathing heavy and sounded exhausted?"

"Maybe."

Anna laughed. "You're my best friend, Janine, but don't expect me to share the details of my honeymoon with you." Her gaze drifted back to the man behind the curtain. "Let's just say that Rafe is everything I thought he'd be, and more."

"All right!" Janine laughed as well. "Now, that sounds like a woman on the receiving end of a great honeymoon. So, why don't you give me a hint about where Rafe took you? I'm thirty-three and stand a better chance of being struck by lightning and eaten by a rabid shark than I do of going on a real honeymoon. The best I can hope for is a *few* steamy details so I can live vicariously."

"Live vicariously through someone else," Anna countered.

"Ah, come on. Just a few details. Are you out on a boat in the middle of a lake, sipping virgin daiquiris and rubbing each other down with coconut-scented suntan oil?"

It was a typical Janine-type question, but for some reason, it gave her another of those nasty jolts. Like the one at the altar. Anna wanted to push it aside but couldn't. Maybe jolts and uncomfortable feelings were now the status quo. And maybe blind trust was a thing of the past.

"Well?" Janine prompted. "Are you at the lake?"

"Not quite." They were in a tiny bathroom with

the sticky steam and the scent of Rafe's deodorant soap in the air. "Suffice it to say we're alone."

"Aah. Sounds like heaven with a capital *H*. And since you don't need a friend for that, I'll just say goodbye. Enjoy every minute of it, Anna. Rafe and you deserve this."

"Bye." Anna listened to Janine's reminder about picking up the iron pills, clicked off the phone and got to her feet.

Sounds like heaven with a capital H.

Yes. It would have been if Rafe's memory were in full working order. Then she wouldn't have been sitting on the floor gawking at him while he took a shower. She would have been in that steamy, hot water right along with him. They would no doubt be kissing.

Among other things.

Her hands would have been all over his hard, soap-slick body. And his hands—those magic hands— would have been all over her. Body against body. It certainly wouldn't have been doubts and regrets she would be feeling. No. It would have been heaven with a capital *H*.

Anna had to fan herself.

Great day. The fantasizing had to stop. If she didn't get her mind off Rafe's hot, soapy, hard body, she might self-combust.

Or something.

Talk about the ultimate irony. She'd waited all her

life to be with a man like Rafe. Now, here she was married to him. Madly, hopelessly in love with him. And yet she couldn't have him.

Fate really did have a twisted sense of humor. Too bad it didn't cool the flames that her fantasizing had fanned. She ached to touch him. Ached to kiss him. And just plain ached for everything else that only Rafe could give her.

He turned off the shower, and one nicely muscled, tanned arm reached out from the curtain. He snagged the towel from the rack and stepped out, bringing some of the steam with him. It seemed to rise off his body.

Rafe knotted the towel at his waist. "A problem?" he asked.

Anna opened her mouth to tell him no, but nothing came out. No sound. Not even a syllable. Nothing.

Mercy.

If she thought the view behind the shower curtain was tantalizing, it was paltry compared to the view she had now. Rafe was only inches away. He was wet all over. Practically naked. With drops of water sliding down his face. Down his neck. Down his lean, muscled chest. Down his equally lean and muscled stomach.

And down the rest of him.

Only that fluffy white towel prevented her from getting the greatest of peep shows.

"That was Janine," Anna explained after she remembered how to speak. And breathe. Good grief, had the air been sucked out of the room? "She called. Good thing I brought the phone in here, or else I might not have heard it ring."

He stared at her a moment, studying her. Thank God he couldn't read minds.

Or hormone levels.

Anna firmly reminded herself that this wasn't really Rafe. Too bad, though, that all those blank spots were trapped inside the face and body of the man that she loved. A man she wanted. And it was also too bad that the want suddenly felt a lot like need.

"I'm sorry about the close quarters," he finally said. "I just didn't want to risk you being alone while I was in here." He combed his fingers through his hair. It fell into place as if he'd just come from the barber. "I needed a shower, and I didn't think you'd care to join me."

Her throat clamped shut. Not the best time for that to happen. Nope. Her silence must have alerted Rafe because his gaze landed on her.

He didn't move, but the narrow space between them suddenly seemed to vanish. Anna couldn't take her eyes off him, and she stood no chance whatsoever of hiding the attraction she felt for him.

"You look…" Rafe shrugged. "Interested."

Oh. Maybe because she was. She was interested in the worst kind of way.

Anna decided she could lie and flat out deny it. Or she could take the ostrich approach and bury her head in the sand. But in the next couple of days, there would probably be other incidents just like this one. So maybe it was a good time to get a few things straight.

"I was *interested* the first time I saw you," she told him, trying to keep her tone clinical. "And I obviously stayed interested, or I wouldn't have said yes when you asked me to marry you. But it's not the same now. I mean, you're not the same. I'm not the same."

The clinical tone went south. God, she was babbling like an idiot and still hadn't gotten her point across. If there was a point.

Without taking his gaze from hers, Rafe came closer. "I'm willing to bet the attraction between us is the same as it's always been. I'm just at a different stage of the ball game than you are, that's all."

Anna took a step back, then another, but the closed door stopped her from going any farther. The look he gave her matched the heat of the steam lingering in the air. It also did an effective job of carving away at what little resolve she'd managed to hang on to. Her brain didn't quite grasp the notion that this was a man she couldn't have.

"You've got memories," he continued, his Texas drawl kissing the words. "But I've got a good imagination to fill in all the blanks."

She laughed. A burst of nervous energy. "That's a dangerous combination."

"You bet it is."

Because he was so close, she could see the struggle going on in his eyes. There was raw attraction, definitely, but it was tempered by common sense.

It was a toss-up as to which would win.

With that water clinging to every inch of him, and his sensuous made-for-kissing mouth so close she could taste it, Anna was no longer sure which outcome to hope for. One thing was for certain—she definitely wanted Rafe.

And he knew it.

Still clutching the towel with one hand, he reached out and skimmed his thumb over her cheek. "I'd rather cut off my arm than hurt you again."

"I know," she managed to say.

Anna did know it, too. Even with everything that had happened, Rafe was an honorable, decent man. A man who just happened to send her body into overdrive.

"But this isn't about hurt," she explained. "It's about everything else."

And she still wasn't making any sense!

"I lied to you," Rafe admitted. "So, I don't expect you to just get over that because we've got the hots for each other."

The smile came before she could stop it. It was

nerves. All nerves. She blew out a long breath of frustration. "This is hard for me."

He lifted an eyebrow. "Me, too, darling," he drawled.

That cocky grin returned in full force. She felt the impact of it, and of his dimples, all the way to her toes.

Anna clamped her teeth over her bottom lip to keep from smiling again. Part of her wanted to throttle him for making her remember why she'd fallen in love with him in the first place. Another part wanted to reach out, take hold of him and never let go.

Fighting back his own smile, he leaned in and brushed his mouth over hers. "Trust me, I know a little bit about torture. In the past four days, every time I kissed you, I knew it couldn't go any further than that." His lips touched hers again. "I wanted more. And I didn't have to rely on my memory to tell me that."

"Rafe—"

That was as far as she got. Anna didn't know whether to ask him to stop or beg for another kiss. Somewhere between the time he stepped out of that shower and now, she'd lost the battle with right and reason.

He slid his hand around the back of her neck. "Was that a no?" he asked.

But he knew the answer. Anna could see it in the

depths of those cool green eyes. There was nothing about her body language or expression that was saying no.

"I've been trying to talk myself out of this," he whispered.

"Me, too."

"Yeah, and neither one of us is doing a very good job of it."

He was *so* right.

Rafe moved against her. Softly. Body against body. Until she was pressed between him and the door. Everything slowed. Like a lazy, hot breeze. It swirled around her until all she could see and feel was Rafe.

"My memories of you are somewhat limited, but you know what I remember about that first time I saw you in the colonel's office?" he asked.

Unable to speak, she shook her head.

"I remember your hair. It was shiny. And your face—the way it lit up the whole room. It was like you had eaten a whole constellation or something. Honey, you were sparkling." Her breasts brushed against his bare chest and sent her pulse out of control. "But what really got me was your smile."

"My smile?" she repeated. Sweet mercy, she sounded asthmatic. And she couldn't think. Her body was on the verge of begging him to take her where she stood.

"Yeah." He slid his hand to her chin, caressing

her bottom lip with his thumb. "You looked up when I walked into that room. Our eyes met. And you smiled at me. Best damn smile I've ever seen, and I promise you, I've seen some smiles in my lifetime. I remember wondering if you tasted as good as you looked."

He held that long, lingering gaze a moment longer before his mouth came to hers.

Like everything else Rafe McQuade did in life, the kiss was potent and thorough. But surprisingly gentle. Anna felt herself melt against him. The heat of his mouth roared through her and ignited a raging hunger that only he could satisfy.

There was a good reason why Rafe was the only man she'd ever given herself to, and that kiss reminded her of it. He was truly the only man she'd ever truly wanted. Or loved.

Breathing hard, he pulled back and shook his head. "Know what? I was right. You do look as good as you taste."

That did it. The phone slipped from her hand and clattered onto the wet tile floor. Anna threw her arms around him and returned the kiss.

Their mouths came together, adjusted. Took. And claimed. Anna did the same with her body. She pressed herself against him, taking in his warmth and the feel of his corded muscles.

It was perfect. Like coming home.

She slid her leg along the outside of his. Rafe

didn't let it stay merely a caress. He caught on to the back of her knee and positioned it so it cradled his hip. It also did an effective job of bringing the centers of their bodies into direct contact. *Very* direct contact. She felt him hard and hot as he pushed against her.

Anna sucked in her breath. Felt the heat surge within her. She fought to pull him closer, until they seemed one.

But that wasn't enough.

He took that fire bath of kisses to her ear and spoke against her skin. ''I'm willing to bet my prize Harley that you're, uh, as uncomfortable as I am.''

''Oh, yes.'' Her body screamed for more, but she forced herself to remember this shouldn't be happening. Even if she could forget the part about Rafe's memory loss, she couldn't forget all the danger lurking around. ''But this probably isn't the best idea we've—''

He stopped her with a kiss and continued until Anna didn't think she had an ounce of breath, or willpower, left. Just when she was ready to strip off that towel, Rafe tore his mouth from hers.

''This is not easy for me to say, Anna, but you're right about this not being a good idea. I'd be lower than dirt if I made love to you while you still have so many doubt about me.''

''Doubts?'' Anna questioned. ''What doubts?''

He smiled and groaned. ''That's the fire in your

blood talking, so I'll just grit my teeth and pretend you didn't say it. You have doubts, all right, and I don't want to take anything from you that you can't give willingly.''

She cursed. He was right. It was the lust talking, and with everything so unresolved in their lives, making love should be the last thing on her mind.

''Tell you what, though, darling,'' Rafe whispered. ''Here's Plan B. I keep on this towel but do something about your discomfort.''

He slid his hand over her breasts, to her stomach. And lower. Each slippery caress stole her breath.

Rafe stopped, then added some well-placed pressure right on the zipper of her jeans. ''So, what do you say? Want me to take the edge off for you?''

''I can't—''

''Trust me, I'd enjoy it as well. Not quite as much, mind you.'' He flashed those dimples. ''But I'd love to find out if you look as good as you taste when I send you flying straight to the stars.''

''Ooh.'' She groaned.

As offers went, it was the most tempting one by far she'd ever received. But while it might give her some temporary relief, it wouldn't solve anything, and it would complicate an already complicated situation.

With plenty of regrets and with some forced deep breaths, she stepped away from him.

Rafe ground his forehead against the door. "That's what I figured you'd say."

He pulled in several generous breaths of his own and reached for a pair of boxers he'd placed on the vanity. He slid them on beneath the towel. Anna tried not to notice that he was fully aroused, but it would have been impossible not to notice *that*.

"I have to know something," he commented. The towel slid from his waist and fell to the floor. "Did I make the experience as pleasurable as possible for you that afternoon I took your virginity?"

She'd already opened her mouth to answer, but he cursed and grabbed his holster off the vanity.

"Where? How?" he demanded.

It took her a moment to realize he was responding to something that someone had said into his earpiece. Sheldon, probably. And from the look on Rafe's face, it wasn't good news. Just like that, the passion evaporated, and in its place crawled the cold, hard fear.

Rafe flipped off the light, wrapped an arm around her and hauled her to the floor.

"How the devil did that happen?" he demanded.

Anna braced herself. But there was no way she could have braced herself for what she heard. It was the sound of a low-flying plane.

"I take it that's not one of ours?" she asked.

"No. And neither are the men who just parachuted out of it."

Oh, God.

While she sat stock-still in the dark room, the sound grew closer. And closer. Anna pulled in her breath and waited.

It didn't take long, mere seconds, before she heard the first shot.

Chapter Seven

Gunfire pelted the cabin. Bullets tore though the thick logs and penetrated the interior near the ceiling. It was a barrage of ammunition, and Rafe had no doubt that it was coming from at least three automatic weapons.

Somehow, he managed to get the bathroom door open, and he shoved Anna into the pitch-black hallway, away from the windows. He followed on top of her, sheltering her from the flying debris.

"What should we do?" she yelled.

"Stay down until Sheldon and the others intervene."

It wasn't much of a plan, but at the moment it was the only one Rafe had. He had to trust that the team positioned at the end of the road would soon respond, and that the trained combat specialists along with Sheldon could put a stop to what was happening. If not, if the primary defense failed, he was armed and ready for a secondary assault.

Rafe resisted the instinct to join the fight then and there. He didn't dare leave Anna alone and unprotected. Instead, he forced himself to concentrate on the method of attack itself. Simple but effective. A light aircraft. Three armed men parachuting into the area at night. They were likely members of Quivira's group of rebels. God knows how they'd managed to avoid the detection equipment to get this close, but later he'd find out how they had accomplished it.

He listened to the sound of the striking bullets. And studied the pattern. There was no breaking glass. No concentration of gunfire in the bathroom, where the only light had been on only moments earlier. Just the nonstop blasts of lead through wood.

And that told Rafe loads about their situation.

The gunmen obviously weren't aiming to kill, so that didn't leave many possibilities. They either wanted him. Or Anna. Or both. But they wanted them alive. That meant they were using the gunfire as a distraction and were probably already closing in on the cabin.

"Where the devil are you, Sheldon?" Rafe called out. He levered himself up slightly in case he had to fire.

"Nearby," Sheldon barked into the earpiece. "Hold your horses. I'm trying to establish position here."

Easier said than done. It riled Rafe to the core that the rebels had put Anna's life in danger. Any one of those bullets could ricochet and hurt her or the baby. In hindsight he could see that bringing her here to the cabin had been a huge mistake. Too bad it'd taken hindsight for him to figure out that one.

"Rafe?" he heard someone say in the earpiece. Not Sheldon this time but Luke Buchanan. "We're coming in. Stay down."

"No plans to do otherwise," Rafe assured him.

The gunfire assault continued. It was deafening, but Rafe tried to pick through it and figure out the positions of the rebels. North was his guess. They were clustered on the north side of the cabin. The side that faced the bathroom.

He heard the counterattack a moment later. Buchanan and Sheldon had obviously arrived. Still, the rebels didn't stop firing. Beneath him, he felt Anna's whole body tremble. God, he hated that they'd put her through this. She'd already been through too much already.

A spray of bullets slammed into the narrow window at the end of the hall. Glass burst through the air and landed on his back and legs.

"The angle of shots changed," Rafe mumbled.

Damn it. It was wrong. All wrong. And it blew his theory that the rebels were just trying to distract them. Unless...

Rafe put that thought on hold when a round of fire rocketed through the living room.

With his arm still looped around Anna, he dragged

her forward to the hall storage closet. He opened the door, pushed Anna inside and positioned himself in front of her. Rafe braced himself to fire.

The shots continued. Only lower. No more bullets near the ceiling. Someone was aiming directly at the floor, and there wasn't a thing he could to stop it.

Anna mumbled something he couldn't understand. Something about the baby. She was scared out of her mind, no doubt about it. He was scared, too. Not for himself. But for her and his child. Somehow, he had to get them out of this alive.

More shots blasted through the bottom logs of the cabin. Several slammed into the old porcelain bathtub and toilet. Since the shots were coming from multiple directions at once, maybe that meant the team members hadn't been able to contain the rebels. The alternative wasn't something he wanted to consider yet, but he prayed to God it wasn't friendly fire that was coming so close to killing them.

The shots tapered off. Rafe kept count and timed the seconds in between until there was nothing but silence. He didn't dare move yet. He waited for a signal from Sheldon and Buchanan.

"Please tell me it's over," Anna whispered, her voice shaking.

God, he wished he could do that, but he couldn't. It was a worthless consolation, but Rafe reached behind him and touched her face. "I don't know yet."

The silence closed in around them. For Anna, it

must have been smothering. Rafe had been trained to react to situations just like these, and he was damn good at his job. But there was just one little problem with that training. He'd never before had a scenario where he had to protect someone who happened to be carrying his child.

"I'm coming through the front door," Buchanan informed him. "Don't shoot."

"That better mean an all clear," Rafe countered.

"It does. For now."

Like the caress he'd just given Anna, that comment wasn't exactly reassuring. Maybe *for now* would last long enough so that he could get Anna out of there.

When the doorknob moved, Rafe got to his feet, but he kept his weapon aimed. He kept it aimed even after he saw Buchanan in the doorway.

Buchanan eyed the raised gun. "Trying to tell me something, Rafe?"

"No. I just want answers." And more than that, he wanted that nagging feeling in the back of his mind to go away. Something was wrong. But what? "What the heck just happened out there?"

"I'd like to know the same thing." Buchanan didn't holster his weapon, either, when he stepped inside. "Somebody jammed our equipment for a couple of minutes, just long enough for that crop duster to get past us."

"Us?"

''Me and Colonel Shaw. We were the team at the bottom of the hill.''

That should have made Rafe feel a lot better.

It didn't.

''How's Anna?'' Buchanan asked.

''I'm fine,'' she assured him. ''But I'd very much like some answers.''

Buchanan didn't have time to respond because Colonel Shaw stepped inside the cabin. Like Buchanan, he wore a dark battle-dress uniform—a BDU—and was armed to the hilt. They'd obviously been prepared for a fight.

Rafe gripped Anna's wrist and helped her to her feet. Because she didn't look too steady, he slid his arm around her waist and held on.

The colonel made a cursory glance of Rafe's attire. Only then did he remember he wore just his boxers. He was lucky to have on those. If the attack had happened moments earlier, he would have had on a towel.

''So, what happened?'' Rafe asked.

Shaw shook his head. ''Three men are dead. We had no choice but to take them out.''

''Oh, God,'' Anna whispered. ''Were they Quivira's men?''

''I wouldn't count on it,'' Nicholas Sheldon explained as he came through the door. He swatted the dust and bits of leaves off his camouflaged pants. ''I managed to get some images just as the plane came into view. I'll check it out as soon as I can get back to the bunker, but I think we're dealing with the rival faction here.''

Maybe. Rafe didn't intend to buy that scenario, hook, line and sinker. The angle of the shots told a powerful story. The first shooters had wanted them alive. The second hadn't.

''These guys didn't have kidnapping on their minds,'' Sheldon continued. ''They were aiming to kill.''

''So, you think this is *the* rival faction?'' Rafe asked, keeping his other thoughts to himself.

Shaw relaxed some of the tension in his face and walked toward them. ''We can get into all of that later, Rafe. Anna looks like she needs to sit down.''

''No,'' she snapped. ''Sitting down won't steady my nerves. I'd rather know the truth.''

Rafe wanted to give her a round of applause. The woman sure had backbone. But he saw the steely look in the colonel's eyes. There was something that Shaw didn't want her to know. Maybe that just didn't apply to Anna, either. Maybe there were things Shaw was keeping from him.

Colonel Shaw reached out and took Anna's hand. ''Some of the things that went on out there are classified.''

''Then give me the *official-use-only* version,'' she insisted. She pulled her hand from his and stepped back. "Because the way I see it, this just got official, and I have a need to know."

Despite everything, Rafe almost smiled. She definitely had backbone.

"All right." The colonel reholstered his weapon and nodded. "We have reason to believe that Victor O'Reilly has joined in on this fight."

"O'Reilly," Rafe repeated. And then he cursed. It wasn't news he wanted to hear, but it sure explained all those stray bullets. Quivira wanted him alive, to retrieve some information about God knows what. But O'Reilly, well, that was a whole different story.

In the simplest terms possible, O'Reilly was an expatriated American scumbag. He was just as powerful. Just as lethal. Just as mean. And he wouldn't hesitate to kill Anna or him if it meant keeping vital information from Quivira. That left Rafe with another question—why didn't O'Reilly want his old rival to get his hands on the information locked in those blank spots of his memory?

"Victor O'Reilly?" Anna questioned. "As in the man who's battling Quivira for control of the same territory in South America?"

"The very one." Rafe didn't have to give Anna biographical details about the man. After all, she'd been caught in cross fire in Monte de Leon between Quivira and O'Reilly's troops. "It could mean that whatever's trapped in my head, O'Reilly wants it to stay there, and he'll kill me to make sure it does. Or maybe he just wants me dead for another reason that I can't remember.''

''Great,'' she mumbled, pressing her fingertips to her mouth. ''Just great.''

Yeah. And if he was in danger, so were Anna and their baby. If Quivira planned to kidnap and use her as leverage, then O'Reilly wouldn't hesitate to do the same. Or worse.

''There's more,'' Shaw continued, looking straight at Anna. ''Sheldon listened in on your call from Janine Billings.''

She shook her head. ''Why?''

Hell. Rafe knew the answer, and he also knew that Anna wasn't going to like it.

''Janine knows Victor O'Reilly,'' Rafe explained, hoping it would sound better coming from him rather than Shaw. ''They were, uh, friends years ago when he was in law school at the University of Texas.''

''Friends?'' she repeated. She sounded calm, but Rafe suspected there were at least a dozen questions going through her head. Ugly questions. And at least one of those questions would deal with why he hadn't mentioned this sooner.

''We've been monitoring her activity for weeks now,'' Shaw added.

Anna motioned toward the splinters, broken glass and other debris that littered the cabin. ''And you think Janine had something to do with this?''

''She left her apartment immediately after she got

off the phone with you. She walked two blocks to a café and is at this very moment having a double latte with a man who has close ties to O'Reilly.''

''That proves nothing,'' Anna snarled.

But it didn't sound as if she completely believed that. Rafe groaned. He hadn't wanted her to learn about Janine this way. From all accounts, Anna and Janine hadn't known each other long but were as close as sisters.

''There's tracing equipment on her phone,'' Buchanan explained. ''We don't know if she put it there or if someone else did. But at this point, we can't take any chances.''

Anna turned to Rafe. ''You knew about this?''

He nodded.

Her eyes darkened. ''You listened to my phone conversation with her?''

''No. But Sheldon did.''

She squeezed her eyes shut and made a shivering sound of anger. ''Any other violations of my privacy that I should know about?'' Anna demanded. She opened her eyes and stormed toward Sheldon. ''How about it? Did you enjoy listening to a private conversation with my friend?''

''Just doing my job, Mrs. McQuade.''

''Anna, the order came from me,'' Shaw assured her. ''If you want to blame someone, then aim in my direction.''

''All right, I will. Know what else? I'll blame you

for the shooting, too. You shouldn't have had us come here. Those rebels nearly killed us.''

''I know, and it's not going to happen again.''

Rafe didn't add a vote of confidence to that, but he intended to be much more vigilant. Maybe he could even convince Anna of that.

''We're leaving here, right?'' he asked Shaw.

''Yes. Get dressed.'' Shaw looked back at Buchanan and Sheldon. ''We go to the backup plan. Prepare the bravo location. We move immediately.''

Rafe knew about the bravo location. It was another cabin at an undisclosed location. Suddenly the term ''undisclosed location'' made him very uncomfortable. If he was about to ask Anna to go anywhere with him, then he personally wanted to make sure it was safe.

He studied each man. Shaw, Sheldon, Buchanan. When it got right down to it, he didn't really know any of them. He'd known Shaw and Buchanan barely a year. A year he didn't even remember. He knew even less about Sheldon.

That made Rafe very uneasy.

Because despite all of Shaw's precautions, reassurances and backups, Quivira or O'Reilly had gotten through what was supposed to have been impenetrable security. And that left Rafe with one serious question.

How?

Chapter Eight

Anna glanced around the tiny cabin. She could probably touch both sides at once if she merely stretched her arms out. If she'd been so inclined. She was too exhausted to test her theory.

There was a sitting area, such that it was. It consisted of a sofa and a lamp mounted on the wall above it. Across from that was a counter that could be loosely construed as a kitchen. There was also a bathroom, and sandwiched above it was a loft-type sleeping area.

"And here I thought the other cabin was small," Anna mumbled.

Still, she wasn't complaining. She hadn't wanted to spend another minute in that place. Every splinter, every shard of glass was a reminder of how close Rafe and she had come to being killed.

"Home sweet home," Rafe said from behind her. From the sarcasm in his voice, he obviously wasn't impressed either with the accommodations of the bravo location.

Rafe eased her into the postage-stamp-size living area so that Luke Buchanan could join them. It was a good thing she wasn't claustrophobic because the three of them took up nearly every extra inch of available space.

Buchanan brought in with him the scent of gunfire and battle. She wasn't sure, but she thought there might be bloodstains on his shirt. Anna didn't want to know whose blood it was.

"I'll need to stay in here with you," Buchanan said. "Sorry, but I'm just following orders. Sheldon and the colonel left the car here in case we have to get out, but they're on foot at the end of the road."

"The road has two ends," Rafe informed him. "Let's hope they're watching both."

Again, she heard the sarcasm in Rafe's voice. Their eyes met for a moment, and in that brief encounter, Anna tried to convey her displeasure about their situation. She was especially displeased about him withholding information about Janine.

Now, if she could just figure out how she felt about that information, then she might be able to figure out what to do. And whom to trust.

God, was it possible that Janine was in on this?

She didn't want to believe it. Janine and she had grown close over the past couple of months. But Anna didn't intend to push anything aside. Not anymore. After all, Janine had never said a word about knowing any South American rebels, and that subject had come up numerous times after her return from Monte de Leon and during Rafe's captivity. It was definitely something Janine should have mentioned.

And then there was that coffee meeting with one of Victor O'Reilly's associates. No, Anna wasn't about to push that aside, even if she couldn't come up with a plausible reason as to why Janine would turn traitor and put people's lives—including hers—at stake.

"Anna and I'll try to get some rest," Rafe announced, not waiting to get Buchanan's opinion about it.

She almost resisted when Rafe took her arm and helped her up the ladder to the sleeping area. Almost. But there was something in his body language and firm grip that made her think he had more than just rest on his mind.

"Careful," he whispered. Rafe put his mouth close to her ear as they sank onto the narrow mattress. "The place is probably bugged."

Anna barely managed to suppress a groan. She'd had her fill of people listening in on her private conversations. Heaven knows if Sheldon had overheard her talking to Janine about the baby. It was bad enough that Shaw knew.

Rafe shut the curtain that separated their bed from the rest of the cabin. It prevented Buchanan from seeing them, but that didn't mean he still wasn't capable of hearing whatever they said. Of course, he might not have to resort to such primitive measures if the place was truly bugged.

"Don't know about you," Rafe whispered, "but I don't have a warm and fuzzy feeling about any of this."

"I agree, but what do we do about it?"

Rafe glanced out the tiny window at the head of their bed. "I'm not sure." He partially shut that curtain, as well. "I guess that depends on how much you trust me."

There was still a thin light coming from the edges of the main curtain so she could see the expression on his face. It probably mirrored her own concern. At the moment, trust was a huge issue between them.

"I'm scared," she admitted, knowing it didn't answer his question. But the truth was she did trust him. A few blank spots in his memory couldn't erase the relationship she'd created with Rafe over the past months. With luck, he'd soon remember that relationship. And her.

"I know, and I'm sorry." Rafe shook his head. "I wish I could do something to make the fear go away."

He lay back, next to her. Side by side. And touching. The closeness stirred other memories within her. Ones that had chosen a bad time to be stirred.

She'd only slept next to Rafe once—in the cellar

in Monte de Leon—and it'd been the most memorable event of her life. This one would be memorable, of course, but for all the wrong reasons. There was no surge of relief that Rafe was safe. No certainty that she'd indeed just been rescued from death itself. There was just the worry that it could happen all over again.

Rafe turned his head to the side so he could whisper in her ear. "How are you *really* doing?"

She heard the inflection and knew he wasn't just talking about her well-being. There was concern for her pregnancy and the child that they'd yet to discuss.

"I'm fine considering everything," Anna admitted. She paused, wondering just how far she should push this. After all, the place was probably bugged. But then, they might not have any quiet, perfect moments for a long time. This could possibly be as good at it would get. "You know, I was as surprised as you were when I found out I was pregnant."

"I can imagine," he mumbled.

There seemed to be a roadblock at the end of that comment, but Anna didn't let it stop her. "I'd planned on telling you on our honeymoon, but I blurted it out when I was holding that gun on you."

"I remember." He paused. "Look, I'm sorry it has to be this way. I mean, I'm sorry you're having to deal with all this uncertainty and the, uh, baby as well."

"You're having to deal with it, too," she reminded him.

"Yeah. I am." He groaned and scrubbed his hand over his face. "All of this would be a helluva lot easier if I just had my memory."

Yes, and then they could get on with their lives. Well, maybe. Maybe the rebels would still want them dead. And maybe their lives would never get back to normal.

"First chance I get, I'll try to get in touch with Cal Rico," Rafe said softly. "He's the one man I know I can trust."

"You really think Rico can find out who's behind this?"

"Maybe." He looked over at her. "All these what-ifs and maybes won't do us a bit of good right now. So, let's concentrate on the things we can do something about. How about let's play 'jog Rafe's memory'?" He picked up her hand and stared at her wedding ring. "Tell me about our first date."

It was probably a ploy to distract her, but Anna didn't care. Every time she closed her eyes, she kept seeing the bullets as they tore through the cabin. Any one of them could have killed Rafe, the baby and her. If she stood a chance of getting any rest, she had to stop thinking about that.

"You took me to a carnival in San Antonio," she whispered. "We rode the roller coaster until I nearly threw up."

He chuckled softly. "And I ate a couple of pounds of cotton candy."

"You did." Anna glanced at him. "Do you remember that?"

"No, I just remember I love the stuff. What else did we do?"

"Let's see." She closed her eyes and let the memories drift through her mind. "We played just about every arcade game there was to play. And you won second place in the mechanical-bull-riding contest."

"Second? I didn't win?"

Anna smiled. Rafe had had the same reaction that night. "There was stiff competition."

He stayed quiet for several moments, and Anna felt the light mood drain away. "I'm sorry I kept that information about Janine from you. Let me just say this—I'm not aware of any more secrets. But from here on out, I'll tell you the whole truth about everything, even if it's something that might upset you."

It was definitely the right thing to say. It made her feel marginally better about their situation. Too bad there were at least a dozen other issues to worry about, and one especially kept pestering her.

She kept her eyes closed, afraid of how he'd react to her question. "If you don't get your memory back—"

"It'll come back," Rafe interrupted.

"And if it doesn't, what then? It's something you have to consider."

"You're asking about us, aren't you? You want to know what'll happen to us if those blank spots aren't filled in?"

"Yes," Anna murmured. But she wasn't so sure she could manage the next part. She took a deep breath first and tried to prepare herself for where this conversation might end. "Will you get a divorce?"

Rafe never hesitated. "No way."

"But—"

He brushed a kiss on her cheek. "Darling, I've already consummated this marriage in my head at least a dozen times. That counts for something."

Maybe. But Anna couldn't rest her hopes on it. If Rafe got his memory back, or even if he didn't, his feelings for her might never be the same.

Never.

They certainly couldn't go back to where they had once been. There was a connection between them. And an enormous barrier.

Anna had no idea which one would win in the end.

"You're thinking too much again." Rafe pulled her into his arms. "Now, get some sleep. You'll need it if I can figure out a way to get us out of here."

Yes. She did need to sleep, but Anna didn't think it'd come tonight. Still, she eased herself deeper into Rafe's embrace and let the night and the safety of his arms take over.

Chapter Nine

The nightmare raced through Rafe's head....

A brutal guerrilla-style ambush in the jungle. It was spliced with images from his own rescue two months later. Fragments of violence that followed a meeting gone bad. He'd been caught in a three-way cross fire between the CROs, O'Reilly's group of rebels and the men from Quivira's forces. A deadly triple ticket that could have easily left him dead.

And almost did.

Rafe had seen the bodies that littered the jungle. He'd studied the intel reports, had memorized them, so he could put identities with some of those dead faces. Quivira's own number-two man, Miguel Ramos. Across from him was Eve DeCalley, an agent from a private research facility, Sen-tron, who'd infiltrated Quivira's group a month earlier as part of Shaw's plan to draw out the rebel leader. The agent's death was a loss not only of life but of valuable information.

Just down the same bloody path lay Quivira's own son. Nineteen years old. Colonel Shaw had to shoot the kid or else be shot. In the end, the rebel leader's son had died along with the others. And in the end, before Rafe could make it out of that hellhole, he'd found himself facing the business end of an assault rifle held by one of Quivira's men.

Rafe still felt the sting of the ropes around his wrists. Even in sleep, he reacted as he'd been trained to react. His body prepared itself for the fight. He wouldn't die. He refused to die.

Evade and escape.

Those were his only options. Anna was safe. A few hours earlier, he'd put her on that transport himself, and somehow he had to make it home where she was waiting for him.

Pain from the brutal beating came back to him in broken, clipped images. The crack of his rib. The taste of his own blood in his mouth. The jab of the needle into his arm.

And there were questions. Always questions. His and theirs. About Shadow Warrior—a synthetic, weaponized strain of a deadly flu virus and its antidote. A virus and antidote that didn't exist outside the walls of the Sen-tron research agency. No one, especially the Alpha Team, had any plans for Quivira to get his hands on it, but Shaw had hoped Shadow Warrior would lure the rebel out.

Quivira definitely wanted the deadly virus to use

against his enemies. But it wasn't the only thing. He wanted the information that Rafe had. It was Quivira's need for the information that'd caused him to fill the needle with the truth serum and shove it into Rafe's arm.

What had he wanted to know?

What?

It seemed there. Just within reach. Rafe felt as if he could almost touch it, but it faded before he could hold on to it.

"Rafe?"

His eyes jarred open. Rafe reached for his gun, but he felt her catch on to him. He almost broke her grip the hard way before he realized whose hands were on him.

"Anna," he whispered.

"You were dreaming." Her voice was a murmur. Soft. Warm. Reassuring. Like the hand she smoothed over his cheek.

"I don't know what he wants," Rafe mumbled. Remnants of the nightmare were still with him. Pieces of violence that wouldn't go away. The images still roared through his head, filling him with adrenaline. "Damn it, I just don't know what he wants from me."

"It's all right. It'll come to you."

Rafe latched on to every gently spoken word. God, did he need them. It didn't seem possible that a woman he hardly knew could make him feel as if everything would be okay. But that's exactly what she did. Maybe that's why he'd fallen in love with Anna in the first place.

She eased closer to him, her movements drowsy and slow. She slipped her hand around the back of his neck and into his hair. Her body brushed against him. And as if it were the most natural thing in the world, her mouth came to his.

Like the rest of the moment, the kiss she gave him was unhurried. The fingers that she trailed down his cheek, barely a caress. But that was all it took to erase the nightmare and make him want her more than his next breath.

Rafe fought through the sleepy haze in his head and tried to figure out if this should be happening. The answer he got was a no. And not just a plain *no,* either, but a resounding one. The timing sucked, no doubt about it.

Still, it felt damn good to hang on to what she was offering him.

He didn't hear anything suspicious. Just the drone of the air conditioner at the back of the cabin. Buchanan had turned off the lights in the main part of the cabin hours ago, just before Rafe allowed himself to doze off.

Rafe glanced out the tiny corner of the window—sunrise was still a half hour away. They were possibly in danger, and he needed to figure out how to get them out of there.

Still, he didn't pull away from her.

He cursed himself. It seemed wrong to take this intimacy from her when he couldn't remember the feelings that'd created the intimacy in the first place. But not all of those feelings were uncertain. He did care for Anna. A lot. That seemed, well, ingrained, as if destiny had paired them and wouldn't have things otherwise.

But just how deep did that caring and destiny go?

"You're thinking too much," Anna murmured against his mouth.

Mercy. The woman tossed his own words at him. He smiled in spite of the battle going on in his head. Too bad that battle didn't do a thing to cool his engines. That one little kiss from Anna quelled every argument he had for putting a stop to this. He wanted her gentle words.

Her touch.

Her mouth.

He wanted *her*.

Rafe gave up the fight that he knew he wouldn't win and hauled her to him.

"Restraint," he reminded himself. As if a mere reminder could stop this.

He couldn't keep the kiss lazy and gentle as she'd done. No way. He dove in headfirst. The energy from the nightmare and the leftover adrenaline fused with the need he had for her. Just her. Memories weren't necessary for him to know that he'd never needed or cared for a woman as much as Anna.

This was all need. All flames. It scared the devil out of him, and yet he wanted it to consume him.

They both fought to deepen the kiss. Her tongue mated with his. His grip on her tightened. They clung to each other. And the need just simply kept on building.

Rafe pushed some strands of hair away from her face and stared down at her. "Did we do this when I made love to you?" he whispered.

"Oh, yes. And more."

Good. So he hadn't just taken her in a flash of heat. How he'd managed not to do exactly that, he might never know. As it was, he had to fight not to take her right then, right there. He couldn't afford to lose himself inside her.

And that's exactly what would happen.

He'd lose himself and forget all about the danger that was still around them. She deserved a lot better than that. So, he had to play this safe even if it drove him out of his freaking mind.

Anna pulled him right back to her, her mouth hungry and hot, and she moved herself against him. He knew what she wanted, what she needed, and cursed the fact that his need matched hers. Too bad his would have to wait.

But he had other plans for her. Rafe undid her buttons and pushed open her shirt.

"Is it all right if we do this?" she mumbled.

"It's better than all right."

He would have liked to take a fire bath of kisses to her stomach and lower, but there was no way he could manage that in the tiny space without making a ton of noise. Logistically, the cabin wasn't a prime location for a long night of lovemaking. Still, where there was a will, there was a way. The will part was a given, and he'd already thought of a way.

He ran his hand over her stomach, and while he kissed her mouth, he opened the snap on her jeans. She reached for his zipper as well, but Rafe stopped her. One touch from her, and he wouldn't be able to think straight. For about a million reasons he needed to keep a clear head. Hopefully, that was possible. With the scent of her arousal all around him and the taste of her in his mouth, it would be a tough fight.

"Did I touch you like this when we made love?" he asked against her ear. He slipped his hand past the opening of her jeans and into her silky panties.

Her breath came out in short, hot bursts, and her grip tightened on his shoulders. "You did."

"How about this?" He went lower. And lower. Slowly. Until he slid his fingers into the wet heat of her body.

"Yes," she managed to say. She arched against his hand. "Definitely yes. I liked it then, and now."

The honest answer was nearly his undoing. It fueled his own heat, but because he had no other choice, he pushed that desire aside. Rafe ran his tongue over her earlobe and matched it with the strokes of his fingers. She gasped softly and frantically sought out his mouth.

He obliged. And kissed her.

She pulled him hard against her. The kiss didn't stop. Neither did the rhythm of his fingers inside her. She lifted her hips off the mattress, deepening the pressure of his touch.

"Did we do this?" he asked, fighting to keep the flames inside him in check.

"We did more. A lot more. It was magic. We were good together, Rafe."

He ached to join her in the most intimate way. To slide into that heat and move with her in an ancient cadence that would send them both over the edge.

But he couldn't do that and keep her safe.

Instead, he did the only thing he could do. He touched. And coaxed. He whispered words, and with each stroke of his fingers, he learned how to pleasure this woman he'd married.

She wrapped her arms around him and buried her face against his neck. "I shouldn't—"

"Wrong. You definitely should," he insisted. Rafe pulled back slightly so he could see her face. "Let me do this for you."

"I'd rather wait until both of us are ready to do this together."

He groaned. It wasn't the best time for that old

philosophy to rear its head. "I'm ready," he assured her. "Make that more than ready, but I just can't give you my undivided attention right now."

"I know, and that's why we should wait."

She slid her hand over his. Stopping him. Unfortunately, the back of her hand rubbed over the front of his jeans. The worst place possible. Other than nearly jumping out of his skin, he damn near embarrassed himself.

Alarmed, she shifted her position so she could look into his eyes. "Did I hurt you?"

"No." Rafe brushed a kiss on her mouth. "Why don't you let me finish what I started here?"

Anna shook her head and rebuttoned her top and jeans. "Believe me, I want that. Well, part of me does, anyway. But this isn't the right time or the right place."

"No. It's not," he confirmed.

She stared at him, apparently a little surprised that he'd agreed so readily. "And all this fire and, uh, whatever, apparently isn't going anywhere. It'll keep until we've…well, it'll keep."

Rafe had already geared up to agree to that as well. Reluctantly so, but he still would have agreed.

However, something stopped him.

Not a sound, exactly. And not even anything specific. It was just the feeling that something wasn't right. He lifted his head a fraction and listened.

She started to say something, but Rafe motioned

for her to stay quiet. He eased back the curtain and looked out into the cabin. Buchanan was on the small sofa beneath them, but his eyes flew open the moment that Rafe's gaze met his.

"Problem?" Buchanan mouthed after a noisy yawn.

"Maybe."

He caught on to Anna's hand and helped her off the mattress. Buchanan got to his feet and met them at the bottom of the ladder. Silently, both men checked out their surroundings. Without releasing his grip on Anna, Rafe went to the door and glanced out the tiny window next to it. Buchanan did the same on the other side of the cabin.

"Anything?" Rafe asked Buchanan.

"Negative."

That didn't do a thing to reassure Rafe. Something was wrong. Too bad he couldn't quite figure out what. There seemed to be a fog thickening in his head.

He put his hand on the doorknob and sifted through the sounds of the predawn. The air conditioner was still running. But what Rafe didn't hear was anything else. No sound of the woods. No sound of anything. And that made the hair stand up on the back of his neck.

Anna yawned and slumped against him. Rafe yawned as well and tried to shake off the dizziness. The dizziness he shouldn't have been feeling.

"I'm getting Anna out of here now," Rafe informed Buchanan.

"My orders are to keep you here."

As if that would stop him. Buchanan moved toward the door, but Rafe just muscled him aside. "Then, you'll have to disobey them because I'm not staying."

Rafe heard it then. The sound that his body had already braced itself to hear. Not the air conditioner as he'd originally thought. No. This was a car engine. And it was too damn close to the cabin.

"Get out!" Rafe yelled.

He threw open the door, pulled Anna out with him and began to run as fast as his feet would carry him. Her steps were sluggish, and he finally lifted her off the ground.

Rafe looked back only to make sure that Buchanan had evacuated. He had. And Rafe saw something else. The car. With a hose running from the exhaust into the cabin.

Someone had just tried to kill them.

And that someone apparently wasn't finished.

Rafe skirted to the other side of an embankment just as the artillery shell blasted through the cabin. Fiery debris launched through the air in every direction. He didn't stop. Rafe kept a death grip on Anna and headed straight for the woods. It might be the only chance they had for survival.

A BULLET RICOCHETED OFF the branches of a dead oak, sending a spray of splinters into the air. Anna ducked her head down, but somehow managed to get her feet on the ground so they could run even faster. She let Rafe lead the way.

She risked a glance behind her. The sun had just risen, but she didn't need the morning light to see the angry coils of black smoke and fire that rose from what was left of the cabin. It confirmed what she already knew—they'd barely made it out of there alive.

Buchanan and the others were nowhere in sight. Hopefully, they'd made it away from the attack, as well. Like them, they were probably running for cover. Anna didn't want to think beyond that.

They scrambled over a rocky outcropping. She saw a cactus, a mound of low-growing, flourishing spikes just as Rafe hurdled himself over it. She hurdled, too, but not before one of the needle-like teeth syringed its way through her jeans and into her leg. She clamped her teeth over her lip to keep from crying out in pain.

More bullets.

These sprayed into the ground around them, kicking up dirt and small pebbles. Rafe shoved her in front of him, keeping a tight hold on her shoulder. He was pushing her to save them both, but in doing so, he had also put himself in the direct path of the bullets.

She thought of the baby. The risk, not just from the bullets but also from the exertion. Thankfully, she still jogged three times a week, and the doctor had assured her that it was all right to continue for months to come. But this wasn't a jog. It was a run for their lives. If she stopped, those rebels would kill them. At least if she ran, they stood a chance. Right now, a chance was all they had.

They hurried through a curtain of thick trees, sending them from the sunlight into near darkness. The air was damp and moldy. It smelled of rotting leaves and other disgusting things. Tree trunks twisted into sinewy coils. There were no animals in sight. No sounds, either, except their gusty breaths and their shoes digging into the spongy ground.

The sweat slipped off Anna's forehead and stung her eyes. Behind her, Rafe maneuvered her in the direction he wanted her to go. She felt limp, but she never stopped moving. To do so would mean surrender, and she had no plans to do that anytime soon. She would survive for her baby's sake.

The cloak of trees didn't last long. As much as Anna had disliked that eerie forest, she'd felt slightly safe there. It didn't last. They soon exited the other side. And were forced to come to a dead stop.

Their chances of survival just went from slim to none.

Chapter Ten

Anna looked down and cursed. Rafe echoed much the same on a harsher scale.

Only inches from their shoes was a steep rock cliff that went straight down at least thirty feet. At the bottom was a sliver of a creek that looked about an inch deep. Jumping into it would be suicide.

"What now?" she whispered frantically.

Behind them, she heard the continuous rattle of gunfire, and it seemed to be getting closer. It would only be seconds before those gunmen tracked them down.

Rafe didn't answer. He moved along the ledge, and Anna followed. Keeping their pace at a quick jog, he kept his eyes angled on the cliff wall, studying. He was obviously looking for something, but she didn't have any idea what.

"Hang on," he warned a split second before he pulled her to the ground.

Rafe began to climb down the rocks toward a bush

that jutted out from the cliff. For a moment, she thought he'd lost his mind, but then Anna saw what had captured his attention. It was a crevice several feet below, and it just might be deep enough to hide them.

Rafe went first. He eased himself onto a narrow lip beside the crevice and grabbed her wrist to help her. She tried not to waste even a second, even though her hands were trembling. It wasn't a good time to realize that she had a fear of heights, but Anna quickly pushed that fear aside and tried not to look down.

Gripping the scrawny bush, she shimmied down the rocks on her bottom until she reached the spot where Rafe was precariously balanced. He tightened his grip on her wrist, shouldered her into the small space and followed right behind her. After he'd sandwiched her inside, he twisted the bush so that it partially hid them.

The gunfire continued, but she couldn't tell how far away it was. Anna stood there praying. Somehow, they had to get out of this alive.

Inch by inch, Rafe positioned himself in front of her, his weapon ready to fire. And they waited.

The minutes crawled by. Anna pressed her face against his back and closed her eyes, hoping it would shut out the noise.

It didn't.

She wasn't sure how long they stood there braced

for the worst and praying for the best. Eventually, the shots tapered off until there was nothing but silence.

"Rafe?" Colonel Shaw shouted.

He was close. Very close. Perhaps just at the top of the ledge. But Rafe didn't move, and he motioned for her to stay quiet.

Anna didn't know how to react to that. So far, Shaw hadn't done a very good job of keeping the rebels away from them. Still, it might be safer with Shaw than forging out on their own.

Might.

But at this point she would trust Rafe before anyone else, including the man she'd known since she was a child.

"Rafe? Anna?" Not Shaw that time but Luke Buchanan. Sheldon joined Buchanan and Shaw, as well, and soon all three men were calling out for them.

Rafe didn't move a muscle. He was as calm as he'd been at the church. Unlike her. She was shaking from head to toe. Anna leaned against him and hoped her legs didn't give way.

The men's voices soon faded until she could no longer hear them. Still, Rafe waited for what seemed a lifetime before he relaxed the grip on his gun and glanced back at her.

"Are you okay?" he mouthed.

Anna nodded. But it was a lie that Rafe must have

seen right through. He turned, adjusting his footing until he faced her.

"You did great," he said. He kept his voice soft and low.

"The day's not over yet. I could still go all medieval on you."

Somehow, he managed a smile. He looped his arm around her waist and carefully eased them both to the floor of the crevice. The sharp edges of the rocks jabbed into her back and side, but it was better than facing gunfire.

Because she needed to touch him, to assure herself that they were both alive, she pressed her fingers to his cheek. "Why does this keep happening?" she whispered. "How do the rebels find us?"

"I'd like to know that information myself. But I think it might be a good idea if we put some distance between us and Colonel Shaw."

"You think he had something to do with all of this?" Anna asked.

"Probably not, but somehow the rebels are tapping into our communications equipment. I've got to figure out a way to stop that from happening. But first we have to get out of here. We'll wait a little longer, until they've given up searching this area. Then I'll see what I can do about finding us a safer place."

Anna didn't want to ask if that was even possible. She was beyond the point of just being tired. In the past two days, she'd slept maybe three hours max.

The fatigue was catching up with her, and she was too weary to think.

"Get some rest," Rafe encouraged when she put her head against his shoulder. He brushed a kiss on her forehead. "I'll wake you when it's time to go."

With her fear of heights, the idea of resting on the side of a cliff didn't especially appeal to her, but going back into those woods frightened her even more. She ran her hand over her stomach and prayed that they could somehow get out of this alive.

"Rest," he whispered.

Anna didn't fight it. She couldn't. The adrenaline rush had come and gone, leaving her too tired to fight anything. She closed her eyes and gave in to the exhaustion.

RAFE CHECKED HIS WATCH, even though the minutes had been ticking off in his head. It'd been a little more than five hours since the last attack, and just slightly less than that since he'd heard anyone from the team call out for him.

He gave his earpiece an adjustment, but there were no sounds coming through it, either. That meant Shaw was out of range.

The area around them was silent. A normal kind of silence. Birds. A gusty breeze. No gut feelings of impending disaster or bad energy in the air.

Hopefully, that meant Shaw and the others were scouring some other area away from the cliff. And that also hopefully meant the latest cadre of rebels were dead. Because soon, Anna and he would have to get the heck out of there. But he didn't want to dodge bullets while he did that. They'd already done enough of that for one day.

Rafe rubbed his thumb over her cheek when she mumbled something in her sleep. She was obviously exhausted. He sure was. But rest for him would have to wait. Things could get much worse before they got better.

What he needed was a damn good plan. And fast. He'd already taken what he hoped was the first step in accomplishing that. Shortly after Anna had fallen asleep, Rafe had phoned Rico's emergency number and left a message about what had happened and asked his friend to call him ASAP.

Of course, if Rico was deep undercover—which he almost certainly was—then "ASAP" might not be for days. Still, it was a chance Rafe had to take. Rico possibly had information that would clear up a few things, and if not, he could at least get them moving in the right direction.

Anna stirred against him, snuggling deeper into the curve of his arm. "Baby," she whispered.

Yes. Funny that she should mention that. Even with everything he had to work out, Rafe couldn't quite get his mind off the baby.

Anna probably hadn't realized that someone had pumped carbon monoxide into the cabin. He'd have to tell her, of course, and he didn't need memories to know that it would frighten her even more than she already was.

Judas.

He had no idea how much of the potentially lethal exhaust they'd inhaled, but as soon as possible Anna would need to see a doctor to learn if it'd had any effect on the baby.

Effect.

The word put a huge knot in his throat.

He eased his hand over Anna's stomach. Over their child. He hadn't wanted to think much about the baby for fear it would break his concentration, but his concentration had seemed practically nil since his return from South America. And now he had to consider that the last attempt on their lives had done something much more than scare them or eat away at their peace of mind. It might have harmed their baby.

As if she'd sensed his thoughts, worry lines bunched up Anna's forehead, and a soft groan left her mouth.

Heaven knew what demons she was wrestling because of this. She'd been through way too much since Monte de Leon. Rico had told him a lot about the day Rafe had rescued her from an abandoned hacienda. If Rafe concentrated very hard, he could almost smell the scent of the cellar where he'd found her. But maybe that was wishful thinking.

God, he wanted to remember.

That was also the day he'd made love to her. Not the best location for such a momentous occasion. A sweltering cellar. The rebels battling it out all around them. Fear. Adrenaline. Relief. Yet, somehow Anna and he had come together and made love. Then he'd asked her to marry him as he put her on the transport that would carry her home.

"Two months ago," he said under his breath. In a cellar with a loaf-size window on the back wall. A two-by-four barricading the door. A rumpled blanket on the floor. And Anna reaching for him. He'd come there to rescue her and send her home.

Saving beautiful photographers is what I do best.

"What?" Anna eased open her eyes and looked up at him. "Did you say something?" she whispered.

Rafe stared at her a moment, trying to figure out if the memory was real or if it was something others had filled in for him. "Just talking to myself."

She glanced down at his hand that was still on her stomach. Her eyebrow lifted a fraction. Rather than say something he didn't want to say, Rafe eased his hand away.

Disappointment went through her eyes. Still, she didn't voice it.

Stretching and making soft sounds of discomfort, Anna sat up but winced when she looked out from the cliff. "How long do we have to stay here?"

Good question. And Rafe hoped he had a good

answer. No matter what he did, it was a gamble. A gamble with Anna and his baby's lives. Still, it was just as dangerous to stay as it was to go.

"We'll need to move soon," he told her. "There's a storm coming in."

She looked up at the sky, at the thick curtain of metal-colored clouds. "Wonderful. Just what we don't need." She pursed her lips for a moment. "You'd think eventually something has to go our way, wouldn't you?"

He could only hope.

The phone clipped to his jeans rattled softly, and Rafe answered it, praying it was the one person he wanted to speak with.

It was.

"Rafe," Captain Cal Rico greeted. "I got your message. Let me guess—this call doesn't have anything to do with you needing love advice for your honeymoon?"

"You got that right." Rafe kept his voice to a whisper and continued to keep a vigilant watch around him. "Is this a secure line?"

"Secure enough."

In other words, someone might be listening. That meant Rafe wouldn't give away his position. "Shaw tells me that it's O'Reilly's men after us, but I'm not so sure."

"O'Reilly, huh?" Rico questioned. "Could be. He slipped into the country a couple of days ago."

That didn't surprise Rafe, but he had to wonder why he hadn't already heard this from Shaw. "Did O'Reilly come in by accident or design?"

"Maybe both."

It wasn't the solid assurance Rafe had hoped to hear, but what else was new? "Does that mean we've got a problem with security?"

"If I were a betting man—and I occasionally am—then I'd say, yes. But now you want a name to go with that burger and fries, huh?"

"A name would be nice. Then I'd know what I'm dealing with."

"You're dealing with a weasel, Rafe. A deadly, slimy one. Sorry, though, I can't give you a name, but I've got two theories. Wanna hear them?"

Rafe looked at Anna. Concern, and hope, was all over her face. Maybe by the time he finished with this call, he'd know what they were up against. And knowing that would help him decide what to do next.

"I definitely want to hear what you've got," he told Rico.

"Here's a tasty little tidbit that may mean nothing. Or everything. The Office of Special Investigations just opened a tab on two Alpha Team members, Luke Buchanan and Nicholas Sheldon. Seems Buchanan came into a rather large sum of money that he's buried several layers deep in an overseas account."

Buchanan. Well, Rafe damn sure didn't trust him. But then, Buchanan had been in that cabin with him.

He'd sucked in as much carbon monoxide as they had. Not very smart unless he'd been double-crossed as well. Or maybe Buchanan had taken safety measures that Rafe didn't know about.

"You think Buchanan is on O'Reilly's payroll?" Rafe asked.

"Either that or someone wants us to believe he is. But Buchanan's not the only potentially smelly weasel in the middle of this. I dug up something about Nicholas Sheldon that had bells the size of Texas going off in my head. Remember Eve DeCalley?"

"Is that a trick question? Of course, I do." Security Specialist Eve DeCalley. Just minutes before Rafe had been taken hostage, Eve had been killed during that ambush. Just about everything that could go wrong did that tragic day. Much like now. "What does Sheldon have to do with Eve?"

"They were lovers. Sheldon might be ticked off in a huge sort of way that Eve died while following Shaw's orders."

It was an interesting connection, but in Rafe's mind, a loose one. Most of the civilian security specialists knew one another since they were all from the same private research facility, Sen-tron. And they all knew the dangers they faced with each mission. Still, Rafe didn't plan to discount the connection. He didn't plan to discount anything.

"And what about Shaw?" Rafe asked. "You got anything on him?"

"No. But here's my advice for what it's worth. Don't trust any of them. Too much has gone wrong with this whole damn operation for someone not to have their fingers where they shouldn't be."

"I agree." Rafe did a quick scan of the area. He needed information, but not at the risk of someone sneaking up on them. Too bad there were too many places to hide.

"I wouldn't mind speaking with Quivira to get his take on things," Rafe continued. "Hell, he might even be able to explain why O'Reilly's gotten in on this. Think you could get him a message so I can try to set up a phone call? I'd like to feel him out and see if he'll tell me what information he's looking for from me."

"You think that's wise?" But Rico didn't let him answer. "I guess it's hard to figure out what's wise or foolish at this point. I'll see what I can do about Quivira, but I can't blow my cover."

"Understood. Thanks."

"By the way, how's Anna?"

Rafe glanced at her again. She looked worn out. And incredibly beautiful. How the heck could she manage that? "She's holding up."

"Um, has she said anything about her, well, state of health?"

The vaguely worded question wasn't so vague since Rafe knew how Rico's mind—and investigative process—worked. Rico had no doubt checked into Anna's whereabouts the past two months. And he'd likely learned that she was pregnant.

"We've talked. She's doing as well as can be...expected," Rafe answered.

"Good. I didn't find out until the day of your wedding, but I knew Anna wouldn't keep something like that from you for long." Rico paused. "Are you okay with it?"

"I'm gettin' there." Somehow, his feelings about the baby had gotten mixed up with everything else. Hard to sort through a jumble of feelings when people kept trying to kill them. "I'll be a whole lot better when Anna's safe. Help me out with that any way you can."

"Will do. But the water's a little dangerous this time of year, so be extra careful."

Rafe picked up on that clue, as well. It was a reference to Rico's houseboat at Canyon Lake, a place only about ten miles away. If they pushed themselves, they could be there before nightfall. And hopefully before the storm moved in. The houseboat had a security system, and even better—Rafe had the access codes to get inside. It'd be an ideal hiding place until he could figure out their next step.

"What'd Rico say?" Anna asked after Rafe said goodbye and hung up.

He gave her the condensed version, not mentioning the part about Rico's knowledge of the pregnancy. Rafe checked his watch again. "We need to move. We have to secure another position."

She nodded, not even questioning him. Rafe almost wished she would. That blind trust didn't make him feel any better about what he had to do.

He helped her from the crevice and got them both back on top of the cliff, all the while thinking that they didn't dare stay out in the open long. The gunmen who'd attacked the cabin might be dead, but no doubt there were others ready and willing to try the same thing.

Rafe moved them into the shelter of the woods. It took him a couple of minutes, but he finally found the catbird seat that they needed. A clump of dense cedar shrubs. The ground around them was littered with dead leaves. It gave a perfect view of the cliff while providing them with a hiding place.

"We'll be here for probably a couple of hours," he said.

She went from looking drowsy to wide awake. "Here? But it's still close to those cliffs."

"Yeah." And that's the reason he'd chosen it. "Trust me. It'll be all right."

Anna glanced at the woods around them. "You sure about that?"

"As sure as I can be about anything." Rafe helped her into the shrubs and followed in behind her. He covered them both with the dead leaves before he unclipped his phone from his belt. "I need to call

Colonel Shaw. I need to figure out exactly whose side he's on.''

Alarm went through her eyes. "And how do you plan to do that?''

"By playing a game that I hope we win.'' He pressed in the emergency numbers, and Shaw answered on the second ring. "It's me,'' Rafe said.

"Where are you—''

"Anna and I are safe. For now. But I need to get her out of here immediately.''

"Of course. Give me your location.''

"We're about a mile and a half east of the bravo site on the west face of a limestone bluff.'' It was a lie. A necessary one.

"All right. Let's see what I can do.''

Rafe listened while the colonel worked out the details with Buchanan. When he finished, Shaw assured him that help was on the way. To the west face of the bluff. Anna and he were on the east side, where they'd hopefully see if *help* would indeed arrive.

"What about the gunmen?'' Rafe asked Shaw.

"Eliminated. They were O'Reilly's men.''

Judas. So, they were right back in the middle of a civil war. Quivira and O'Reilly had brought their battle to the States. It really didn't matter at this point if Quivira wanted him alive. O'Reilly didn't. Besides, Quivira wouldn't hesitate to kill him as soon as he got the information he wanted.

Rafe issued a hasty goodbye to the colonel, hung

up and clipped the phone back onto his belt. "Well, I just set the game in motion," he said to Anna. Maybe it wouldn't blow up in his face. "I gave Colonel Shaw directions to a bogus site, a site we'll be watching carefully to see who shows up."

"How safe is this game?" she asked.

"I don't know. I wish I could promise more, but I can't."

She gave a frustrated sigh. "I'm not blaming you. I'm blaming Quivira and O'Reilly. But no matter who's at fault, I just need this to be over."

"Yeah." Because she looked on the verge of losing it, he touched her cheek and rubbed gently.

The gesture obviously didn't soothe her as he'd planned. "When will you tell me what else is wrong?"

He hadn't realized he'd been that obvious. But then, Anna probably knew him better than he knew himself. He couldn't tell her about the possible harm to the baby. Not now. He couldn't risk how she would react to that.

"I remembered the cellar in Monte de Leon," he softly explained. "The window. The blanket. You told me that you loved me."

It wasn't a lie—Rafe had remembered fragments of that afternoon—but it wasn't the source of what was bothering him.

He could feel her staring at him, but rather than

open himself up to questions he didn't want to answer, Rafe motioned for her to stay quiet.

And he burrowed into their hiding place and braced himself for what he prayed wouldn't happen.

Chapter Eleven

Anna hid in the camouflage of damp leaves and waited.

For what exactly she didn't know.

Colonel Shaw was on the way, but maybe he wasn't the only one. After all, Rafe had a firm grip on his gun and had obviously braced himself for something unpleasant. She wanted to believe it was that possible unpleasantness that had created the tension she saw in Rafe's face.

But she wasn't so sure.

Anna replayed the conversation she'd just had with Rafe. He had told her of Rico's suspicions about Sheldon and Buchanan. That part sounded believable and would have troubled him. Rafe had then recounted his memory in the cellar and her telling him that she loved him. He also no doubt remembered them making love. Also believable and perhaps troubling. But none of those things should have put him in such a dark mood.

So, what had?

She had to consider the obvious. The fact they were in danger was enough to sour anyone's mood. Or maybe it was the baby who was responsible. After all, on the other occasions when Rafe had faced danger, he turned into the ultimate silent warrior. However, making love had no doubt reminded him of the child she carried. A child he seemed indifferent about.

Or something.

Anna glanced at him, unable to figure out what was going on inside his head. Rafe was on his stomach, buried in the leaves except for parts of his face and hands. He had his attention focused on the cliff wall, which was exactly where it should be focused.

Because she was still watching him, she saw him mouth a curse. Just like that, she felt the blood rush through her head. Her lungs tightened. Her concerns of his dark mood shifted to one even more serious—staying alive.

Rafe's gaze cut to her for a second, and in his eyes she saw the warning to stay quiet.

She did.

A moment later, Anna heard the soft sound. Not from the other side of the cliff, either. Closer. Much closer. A snap of a twig. Maybe. And maybe a lot more than that.

She pulled in her breath. Waited. Listened.

Nothing.

All she could hear was the breeze rattling through the towering live oaks. Without moving, she checked out their surroundings as best she could. Everything looked as it should. But the prickle was still there, along with the gut feeling that something definitely wasn't right.

When her lungs began to ache, Anna quietly blew out the breath that she'd forgotten she was holding. Maybe there was nothing to see or hear other than what she'd manufactured in her own overactive imagination. After all, if there'd been a breach in security, the rebels would be on the other side of the cliff where Rafe had told Shaw that they were.

Anna had almost convinced herself to relax when she heard it again.

Definitely a snap.

Maybe even a footstep.

Her heart began to pound, the sound echoing in her ears. She forced herself to breathe normally so she wouldn't hyperventilate. Beside her, Rafe didn't move a muscle.

The sounds continued. But they were closer now. Definitely footsteps. Despite the roar in her ears, she could measure the pace of whomever it was walking. Slow, methodical steps. Not from the cliff. But from behind them.

God, from behind them.

They were about to be ambushed.

Choking back a gasp, she forced herself not to

panic. Instead, she tried to assess the situation in the clinical way that she knew Rafe was doing. Maybe Shaw and the others would have approached them from that direction. Maybe. But at the moment it seemed a lot to hope for.

"Que hay?" someone whispered.

A man's voice. Not Shaw's, Luke Buchanan's or Sheldon's. A stranger's. And even though he'd spoken in Spanish slang, Anna knew the phrase meant that someone was inquiring as to their whereabouts. It evaporated any hope that this was a member of the Alpha Team.

And worse.

That question meant there were at least two of them. Quivira's or O'Reilly's rebels, most likely. Men who would most certainly try to kill them.

Anna prayed. She prayed that the men would just pass them by. But the footsteps grew closer. And closer. It was agony waiting. Pure agony. If the rebels saw them hiding, they could easily shoot them before Rafe could reposition himself to return fire.

Questions and doubts raced through her head. Would the leaves and shrubs give them ample cover? Did the men already know they were there? Would this be one of the last breaths that Rafe and she would ever take? She suddenly wished that Rafe and she had at least talked about the baby. That way, she wouldn't go to the grave doubting how he felt.

From the corner of her left eye, Anna saw the

movement. A blur of motion as a man wearing camouflage fatigues darted behind a tree. Thankfully, he
didn't seem to be looking in their direction. He fixed
his attention on the cliff, and he was armed.

The man had hardly gotten into place when she
heard something on the other side of Rafe. She angled her eyes in his direction. He still hadn't moved.
But just outside the clump of shrubs was another
man. Mere inches away. So close that Anna could
smell the sweat on his clothes.

Everything in her stilled, the fear gripping her by
the throat. As a photographer, she'd had a couple of
tense assignments—the one in Monte de Leon top-
ping the others for situations she most likely wanted
to avoid. But this, this was as close to hell as she
ever wanted to get.

The man behind the tree whispered something.
One word. In Spanish. Anna didn't quite catch it, but
the tone was a warning. An alert. God, had they seen
them hiding?

Beside her, she felt Rafe tense. There was no time
for her to react or try to figure out what he planned
to do. His gun spun to the right.

And he fired.

The sound blasted through the silence. Before the
man standing next to them fell, Rafe rolled on top
of her, his back against hers. He adjusted his aim and
fired again.

At a speed that didn't seem humanly possible,

Rafe sprang up from the ground into a crouching position, his feet on each side of her. A split second later, there was another shot.

Anna was no expert in the sounds of gunfire, but the last shot hadn't come from Rafe. Nor had the one that followed. She bit off the scream that nearly made its way past her throat. God. The rebel was shooting at them, and Rafe was literally out in the open.

She looked up at Rafe, frantically checking for any signs of injury, but he moved before she got little more than a glimpse.

"Stay down," he ordered.

With his attention firmly on the man near the tree and with his finger planted on the trigger, Rafe dove out from the shrubs. Rolling over, he came up on one knee and fired. One deadly efficient shot.

Their attacker slumped forward, the gun dropping from his hand onto the ground. It didn't take long, maybe a second, before the man fell, as well.

Rafe latched on to her hand. "We have to leave. There might be others."

Sweet heaven. She hadn't thought of that. Her mind was a jumble of fear and rage.

Rafe gave her one reassuring glance over his shoulder and led her back into the woods. "I'll get you out of here," he promised.

She believed him. Rafe would indeed get her out of there. But would it matter? Would there simply be more gunmen waiting for them wherever they went?

What had just happened took them well past the theory stage that the rebels had some inside help.

They did.

There was no doubt in Anna's mind. What were the odds that the rebels would be headed in the direction of the bogus rendezvous site unless they'd intercepted—or had been given—the information that Rafe provided Colonel Shaw.

The truth sat cold and hard in her stomach. Someone very close to them had turned traitor. And it'd come very close to getting them killed.

Chapter Twelve

Rafe didn't like the hesitation he heard on the other end of the line. He'd just asked Shaw what should have been a bombshell of sorts, but instead of the colonel denying it, all Rafe got was silence.

Damn.

"Well?" Rafe questioned. Cradling the phone against his ear, he peeled off the rest of his drenched clothes and stepped into a pair of pants that he'd found on Rico's houseboat. Thankfully, Rico had kept the boat well-stocked and ready for emergencies. Even the phone was a secure line. "After what I learned, should I be suspicious about Buchanan and Sheldon?"

Outside, rain pelted the tiny windows of the houseboat, and a slash of lightning sent a ripple of static through the phone line. The boat was anchored about a hundred yards off the lakeshore, but that didn't stop it from bobbing. Rafe propped his hip against the counter to steady himself.

"I'm not sure what you're asking," Shaw concluded.

"And I'm sure you are, *sir*." In fact, Rafe was more than sure. And God help him, Shaw better have some answers. The *right* answers.

Anna stepped out from the tiny bathroom, a thick white towel draped around her hair. And little else. She wore just an oversize to-the-knees T-shirt, one of the few garments they'd managed to locate among Rico's things. It reminded Rafe of the barely there nightgown she'd donned for their honeymoon night.

With the fresh scent of the shower stirring around her, and her lack of clothes, her mere presence commanded Rafe's attention. Attention he couldn't spare if he hoped to learn anything from Shaw.

She caught his gaze, and her eyebrow lifted a fraction.

"Colonel Shaw," he mouthed.

She nodded, though he saw the questions in her intense brown eyes. Questions as to whether or not it was a good idea to call anyone connected to the Alpha Team. Rafe was asking himself the same darn thing. Too bad this might be the only way to get answers. Maybe now he wouldn't have to pay too high a price for that information.

"Buchanan and Sheldon have been under a microscope lately," Shaw assured him.

But it didn't reassure Rafe of squat—something he'd already anticipated. And that's why Rafe had used Rico's secure line so the colonel couldn't trace the call. Hopefully, that secure line and the security system on the houseboat would buy Anna and him some downtime until he could figure out what to do next.

"Look, I can't make you trust either man," Shaw went on. "Or me, for that matter. But—"

"Do you trust them?" Rafe interrupted. "And save the part about them being valuable members of your team. I've already got enough useless information to sift through, thank you. What I want to know is would you put the lives of people you cared about in their hands?"

There was another of those long silences. "I'm taking precautions. But the point is that you and Anna are in danger. I need to know where you are so I can get you some backup."

It was the second time Shaw evaded answering him and the third time he had demanded that Rafe tell him their location. And for the third time Rafe brushed him off.

"Do you trust them?" Rafe repeated.

Another pause. "No."

Finally! It'd been like pulling teeth, but Shaw had admitted what Rafe had already sensed.

"Tell me about the money in Buchanan's account," Rafe said, trying a different angle.

"He claims his soon-to-be ex-wife put it there. It's possible. You don't remember her, Rafe, but she's vindictive. She'd pull this kind of stunt to get back at Buchanan, but Special Investigations can't figure out where she came up with the money to frame him. She just doesn't have those kinds of funds. In fact, this divorce has left both of them pretty much broke.''

Ah. And there was Buchanan's motive in a proverbial nutshell. Rafe knew for a fact that Quivira or O'Reilly would shell out big bucks to get a Justice Department agent on their payroll.

That led him to the next question he wanted to put to Shaw. ''So, what does the Justice Department have to say about all of this?''

''That he's a solid agent, but if you don't want him in on this, then he's off the team. The same goes for Sheldon.''

The colonel's tone was a little too placating. Rafe didn't think that was a good sign. Still, he wasn't about to turn down that offer. He did want them off the team. Heck, he wanted them as far away from Anna and him as they could get. He could add Shaw to that list, though, as well.

''Suffice it to say that you need two new team members,'' Rafe continued. ''But that doesn't mean I'll stop being suspicious about Sheldon and Buchanan. And speaking of Sheldon—how about his connection to Eve DeCalley?''

''It appears to be a coincidence.'' No hesitation that time. So, Shaw had at least given it some thought as to how he would respond when Rafe asked. "Sheldon had a few problems after Agent De-Calley's death, but the Sen-tron shrink said he was good to go."

"Pardon me if I reserve judgment awhile longer on that." Rafe's brow furrowed. "I'm not about to trust my life and Anna's on the opinion of a Sen-tron shrink."

Anna gave a crisp, confirming nod and sank down onto the sofa bed. She looked far better than he'd expected her to look. After all, a ten-mile hike through the rain wasn't the best scenario for a pregnant woman.

Maybe that non-exhausted look had something to do with the way that T-shirt skimmed along the curves of her body. Or maybe it was the misty glow she had from the hot shower. And maybe he was unable to get his mind off her simply because this was Anna.

Rafe reached out and skimmed his finger along her cheek. She moved into his touch. Welcoming it. And feeding it at a time when he shouldn't have been touching her.

"Rafe, this renegade attitude of yours won't help Anna," Shaw insisted. "I can get new team members. People that you trust, but you've got to bring her in. Rico should have told you the same."

That comment confirmed what Rafe already suspected—Shaw had somehow learned about their conversation. Hopefully, the man hadn't picked up on Rico's water reference, but just in case, Rafe would check the security system again when he was done with the call. While he was at it, he'd show Anna the escape door that Rico had had installed when he modified the boat.

"You haven't said a thing about the carbon monoxide," Shaw went on.

That immediately put a heavy fist around his heart. Rafe pulled back his hand from her face and stared down at Anna. Her eyes were examining him, and if he wasn't careful, she'd figure out that Shaw was about to discuss something he definitely didn't want Anna to overhear.

He stepped away from her and went to the window to take a cursory glance outside.

"What about it?" he asked Shaw.

"Buchanan tested out all right. No damage. I suspect it's the same for Anna and you."

There was a *but* at the end of that sentence. The baby wasn't out of the woods yet. There was already so much danger to this child, and now this.

"I have to go," Rafe told him.

"Wait! Tell Anna that Janine's called for her a half-dozen times. She says it's important."

Rafe jotted down the number where Shaw said Janine could be reached. "I don't guess you've had a chance to question her about her old friendship with Victor O'Reilly?"

"I did while I had her on the phone. She said it was water under an old bridge, that she hadn't seen O'Reilly in years. I didn't tell her about the tap, because we're still using it to monitor her line."

"So, how did she explain having coffee with one of his henchmen?"

"Janine said she didn't know the man was connected to O'Reilly."

Yeah, right. He'd heard fish stories like that before. "I'll let Anna know she called." And with that, Rafe ended the call without so much as a goodbye.

"Well?" Anna asked the second he clicked off the phone.

She unwrapped the towel, and her hair tumbled in damp strands against the shoulders of the T-shirt. And the tops of her breasts. Man. He hadn't remembered a T-shirt and wet hair ever looking so damn sexy.

Rafe put the phone on the table and forced his attention away from her and all that...sexiness. "Shaw claimed he doesn't believe Buchanan and Sheldon had anything to do with the rebels getting through to us, but he's bumping them off the team, anyway."

She placed the towel over the back of the chair and rubbed her arms. Probably not because she was cold. The room was toasty warm. And getting warmer by the minute. "I guess this rules out Janine, huh?"

"Maybe not. She could still be working with someone else. By the way, she called Shaw and says she needs to speak to you. That it's important."

Anna glanced at the phone. "Maybe I should find out what she wants."

Rafe doubted that Janine had anything on her mind, other than maybe finding out where they were. Besides, with that tap on Janine's phone, it was way too big of a risk. Shaw could listen in on every word and might be able to figure out their location.

"It wouldn't be a private conversation," he explained. Rafe grabbed a bottle of water from the fridge and leaned against the counter.

"Something's wrong. I can see it in your face." She stood and walked to the counter. "What aren't you telling me?"

Rafe lifted a shoulder. "Hey, isn't being chased by two groups of rebels enough to warrant a troubled expression?"

"Sure. But there's something else. Something we've been avoiding for a while." Slowly, she eased back around to face him. Whatever she was thinking, it wasn't about rebels and gunmen. "Rafe, I need to know how you feel."

He gulped down some water, hoping it would take care of his suddenly dry mouth. It didn't. "About what?"

She pressed her hand on her stomach. "About this."

Ah, hell. She'd probably overheard Shaw's comment about the carbon monoxide. Rafe hadn't wanted her to learn that way. He'd wanted to prepare her first and give her reassurance that everything would be fine.

But Anna didn't give him a chance to say anything.

She pulled back her shoulders, and her eyes narrowed. "If you don't want the baby then, damn it, just say so."

ANNA JUMPED WHEN THUNDER pounded through the tiny houseboat, but she wasn't about to let something like a nighttime storm delay this conversation with Rafe. It was long overdue.

"We've been skirting around this since I told you about the baby," she added. Since she needed something to do with her hands, she used her fingers to try to comb out some of the tangles from her shower.

He nodded. Just nodded. He kept his attention focused on the bottle of water in his hand.

Her heart sank. Anna took a deep breath, hoping it would steady her pulse. "I should have said this sooner, but this isn't your responsibility," she offered. "I can raise the baby myself."

It was an out she'd hoped she would never have to give him. But apparently it had come to that after all. During the months Rafe and she had dated, they hadn't discussed having children. Heck, she didn't even know if he liked kids. And this was obviously too much for him to take.

Rafe put the water onto the counter. "Anna, you don't understand."

"I think I do. It shocked me, too, at first. A baby. I hadn't even thought about getting pregnant when we made love—"

He cursed. It was raw and vicious.

The tears instantly came to her eyes. And Anna couldn't blame them just on the hormones. No. This was a horrible ache in her heart. With everything else going on, she wasn't sure she could take Rafe's rejection, as well. He wasn't just her baby's father, he was the only person she could trust.

His head whipped up, snaring her gaze again, and he closed the narrow distance between them with one step. "I swear it's not *that*."

She shook her head, not understanding. "Then what is it, because I need to know—"

"Colonel Shaw told me that O'Reilly's rebels pumped carbon monoxide into the cabin."

Anna had braced herself for almost anything.

Except that.

Rafe pulled her into his arms. A good thing, too, or she might have fallen.

"Oh, my God," she gasped.

"Buchanan tested fine," Rafe explained, his voice a gentle murmur against her ear. "So, you're probably okay, too. And the baby."

"Probably."

It wasn't nearly enough of a reassurance.

He eased away from her and caught her face between his hands. "I didn't want to say anything because I didn't want to worry you. Again, Buchanan's fine, so in all likelihood, you are, too."

She couldn't stop the worst-case-scenario thoughts that went through her head. Anna had no idea of the effects of carbon monoxide on the baby, but it couldn't be good.

God.

It was something else to worry about. Still, she clung to the hope that if Buchanan was all right, then maybe the baby was, too.

"You can be tested," Rafe continued. "I'll try to arrange for you to see a doctor—"

"I thought you didn't want the baby," she blurted out.

He groaned and pressed his forehead to hers. "It was never that. *Never.* And I don't need my memory to know how I feel about this baby."

Relief washed through her, and despite all the other uncertainties, Anna felt the tension drain from her body. She slumped against him, her arms circling his waist. Only after she'd touched his bare skin did she remember that he wasn't wearing a shirt. Hard to forget something like that.

"I tried not to think about the baby," Rafe went on. "I felt I had to concentrate on getting us out of this mess. But it didn't work. There's no way to put something like that out of my mind.''

''I know.'' She almost hated to push this fragile moment, but Anna wanted to know what all of this meant. ''If those rebels weren't after us, and if you had your memory back, do you think, well, would you be happy about the baby?''

Rafe didn't answer her right away. At least not with words. He angled his head so that their gazes met and then slid his hand over her stomach. ''There're an awful lot of ifs in that question, darling. And you know what? I don't need those ifs because I want this baby, understand?''

She saw it—finally. The look in those clear green eyes that Anna had prayed she would see. Rafe wanted the baby. At the moment, she didn't care if that *want* extended to her. She just needed to hear that he hadn't rejected their child.

He touched his mouth to her forehead. Such a comforting gesture. And so welcome. Maybe it was the relief fueled with the passion that already simmered between them. Or maybe it was the fact they were pressed against each other. It suddenly didn't matter why, but Anna felt the air change around them. An instant awareness that they were man and woman.

Their gazes met. It was little more than a glimpse. And Rafe's mouth came to hers. The heat instantly burned through her. A fire that went from a mere spark to a full blaze with just that one kiss.

"We never get this timing thing right," he grumbled.

Funny. It felt right to her. Under the circumstances, it was about as right as right could get. They were alone. And they were as safe as they could hope for. The storm and security system would hopefully keep everyone else at bay. So for all practical purposes, they were the only two people in their entire world.

She gulped in her breath, taking in the taste of him, as well. From day one, she'd wanted him. Not like this, of course. This was a need that had sprung from the intimacy that only being in love with him could create. Anna wouldn't let herself wonder if Rafe remembered those feelings. For now, this was enough. For now, she only wanted to feel.

As if battling her, and himself, Rafe caught her hands with his and pinned them against the wall. His eyes skimmed over her, and in them, she saw both an apology and a blatant invitation.

"Whatever this is between us, it's not a left-brain thing." He cursed under his breath and shook his head as if disgusted with himself. "Logic tells me to stand guard. To protect you. To move to the other side of the room and leave you alone so I can think straight."

"You're right. This doesn't have anything to do

with logic.'' Anna purposely moved against him. Softly. Slowly. A caress. Her breasts against his chest. The center of her body against his. And because she was so close, she heard him hiss out his breath.

''You might have to set those left-brain thoughts aside,'' she whispered. ''What does your heart tell you to do?''

The corner of his mouth lifted a fraction. It wasn't much of a facial adjustment, but he upped the ante of that blatant invitation. ''My heart tells me to do just about everything not dealing with logic. No surprise there, huh?''

Even with that admission, Anna thought he might put duty first and step away from her.

He didn't.

Rafe grasped her wrist and moved her right hand from the wall to his chest. With him guiding her, he slid her palm along the taut muscles that stirred there. And lower. To his stomach.

''You want to play? Okay, let's play,'' Rafe challenged. ''What does *your* heart tell you to do?''

If he thought she would back away, he was wrong.

''My heart tells me to do this.'' Without moving her hand from his stomach or his grip, she leaned in and kissed him. It wasn't tame. It was long and hungry.

''Not bad.'' His breath was ragged, and so was the

sound that simmered in his throat. "If you want my opinion, darling, your heart's in the right place."

It thrilled her that she was able to do that to him. Of course, Rafe could easily do the same to her.

And probably would.

If she got lucky.

He eased her hand down an inch. "So, what do we do about it?" he asked, obviously continuing the seductive game. "How far does this go?"

"As far as you let it."

That sound in his throat broke free, and he groaned. "Anna, I've given this plenty of thought. *Plenty.* Ninety-nine point nine percent of me wants to strip off any underwear you might have on and take you where you stand." Rafe shook his head. "But I honestly can't give you the words that I know you want to hear."

The words—*"I love you."*

No, he wouldn't be able to say that to her. And Rafe wouldn't lie about something like that. But in her heart, Anna knew those words would come when his memory returned. She knew because Rafe had said them to her in Monte de Leon. Even more, he'd meant them.

She kissed him again, hoping it would save her from giving him an explanation. Because this wasn't something she needed to explain. To make sure she got her point across, she slid her hand lower. Over the front of his loose pants. She moved her fingers over him. Against him.

Around him.

He was already huge and hard, and if there had been any shred of hesitation in her body, that would have eliminated it.

He cursed and jerked away from her, but Anna grabbed his shoulders. "You're not going anywhere," she told him.

He gave her a look that stole her breath. Anna didn't have time to ask his intentions. He fisted his hands in her hair and took her mouth. It was like a flash of fire. All she'd hoped for and more.

Her heartbeat raced. Her body hummed. Every inch of her suddenly seemed desperate. Rafe rocked against her. The hard, rigid part of him against the soft, vulnerable juncture of her thighs. He pressed. Moved. Stroked. Until it wasn't nearly enough.

He slid lower, his body pinning her against the wall. He kissed his way down her throat. Down her breasts. Down her stomach. And dropped to his knees.

The kisses didn't stop.

"You're not going anywhere," he said, repeating her words. "Yet."

Looking up at her, he bunched up the T-shirt and grasped her panties. Since she'd washed them in the bathroom, they were still damp, and Anna felt the cool dampness of the silky fabric as Rafe slid them down her legs. He tossed them aside.

Anna almost asked what he had in mind, but it would have been a stupid question. She knew.

She wanted to resist. Well, part of her did. Not because she didn't want this. It wasn't that. She just wanted him to take this activity in the direction of the sofa bed. The other part wanted to take everything he was offering her right here and now. In the end, it was her need for him that won out. She braced herself for whatever he was about to offer.

Rafe leaned in and kissed the inside of her thigh. She hadn't thought it possible, but that caused the flames to burn hotter. Mercy, she didn't know how much of that she could take without demanding a whole lot more of him.

With slow, deliberate ease, he took her knee and moved it onto his shoulder. "You're not going anywhere," he murmured.

The heat from his moist breath caused Anna to whimper. But it was nothing compared to the heat of his mouth. Rafe took. Sampled. Savored. It was beyond a kiss. It was a primitive claim with his mouth on her flesh, and she hadn't thought anything could feel that good.

Somehow, Anna managed to hold his gaze when that trail of kisses ended at the fiery center of her body. Somehow. But soon her vision blurred. Her need rocketed with every new touch.

He caressed her, gently, with his mouth. With his tongue. Gently and yet exactly the way she needed him to touch her.

"Now you can go," Rafe whispered against that feverish heat.

It didn't take much. A simple brush of his tongue. Anna felt herself soar. Soar. Soar. It was like a spear being hurled through the sky. Until everything within her surrendered. It was far more than she could have even hoped to feel, and yet she was desperate to feel even more.

She came back to earth as quickly as she could, and with the hazy flames still stirring around her, Rafe made his way back up her body. He kissed her. And touched. Until it was Anna who was pushing them toward the sofa bed. Wrapped around each other, they landed on the soft cushions.

It took her a moment to realize that the ringing in her ears wasn't passion-induced. Rafe stopped, cursed and gave her a why-the-heck-now look.

"It might be Rico," he muttered, irritation in his voice.

If so, then his timing was positively lousy. Anna tried not to groan. Or kick herself. Instead of allowing Rafe to pleasure her, she should have gotten on that sofa with him minutes earlier. Then they would have both been satisfied.

Rafe reached across to the counter and snatched up the phone. He didn't say hello. Or anything else, for that matter. He just waited. But Anna had no trouble seeing the surprise that went through his eyes.

Her first thought—a horrible one—was that this was news about the carbon monoxide they'd inhaled in that cabin. She got to her knees, fixing her T-shirt along the way.

''Who is it?'' she mouthed.

''Señor Quivira,'' Rafe said aloud, addressing the man on the phone. ''Mind telling me why the hell you want us dead?''

Chapter Thirteen

Rafe forced himself to remain calm. Hard to do when he was finally speaking with the man who was one of the main reasons Anna's and his lives were in danger. He wanted to reach across the phone lines and send this scum to meet his maker.

"Captain McQuade," Quivira mocked. "You left Monte de Leon without saying goodbye. Poor manners, don't you think? It hurt my feelings."

Quivira's voice went through Rafe like a cold, hard freeze. It was a voice that had tormented him for two months. If there was some emotion beyond pure hate, then that's what he felt for this man.

"I didn't care much for your kind of hospitality," Rafe countered. With the phone cradled against his neck, he started to dress in case they had to get out of there fast. "How did you get this number?"

"From someone who thought it would benefit us both if we spoke." There was no trace of the native accent that Quivira used in the presence of his soldiers. Rafe heard the polish and sophistication of Quivira's Oxford education. Not exactly a common man of the common people that he purported to be. "A friend, you might say."

The friend was no doubt Cal Rico, the man who'd spent weeks infiltrating Quivira's organization. Maybe none of this would jeopardize Rico's undercover mission, but it was a huge risk. Since Rico had set things in motion, Rafe intended to get the most he could for that risk.

"I guess you no longer want anything from me?" Rafe asked, going on the offensive. He glanced at Anna when she rose from the sofa. Without taking her attention from him, she slipped her panties back on and reached for her jeans. "Because that's the only reason I can think of for why you'd want to kill me."

"Rest assured, McQuade, I'm not the one who wants you dead. If so, we wouldn't be having this conversation. Victor O'Reilly's men are after you. And why? Because he thinks you've cut a deal with me for some merchandise that your people promised him. Before he succeeds in eliminating you, we need to take care of a little unfinished business."

Yes. Too bad Rafe didn't remember exactly what that business was. His guess was it had something to do with the virus and antidote, but if so, he'd let Quivira bring up the subject.

"Release the hostages, and that business will no longer be unfinished," Rafe lied.

Quivira laughed. "Such boldness. Under different circumstances, I think we would have become friends, no?"

Not in this freaking lifetime. But Rafe kept that thought to himself. "If you're not in a bargaining mood, then we obviously have nothing to discuss."

"Yes." Quivira paused. "And you'd rather be spending time with your lovely bride, Anna."

Rafe had to clench his teeth to stop himself from saying something he'd regret. Just the sound of Anna's name from this man's lips sent Rafe's blood pressure soaring.

"Let's cut through the bull, shall we?" Quivira suggested. "You tell me what I want to know, and you and your colonel will be rewarded with the release of my...guests."

It was tap-dancing time. Maybe if he asked a few more questions, then Rafe would—

"One day I hope you know what it is to feel a father's grief," Quivira hissed.

Damn him. Damn him. Damn him! It took every ounce of his training, every fiber of his willpower and even a soothing touch from Anna's hand for Rafe to maintain control. How dare this man threaten his child. It cut to the core of what scared him most. And Quivira no doubt knew that.

Before he could unclench his teeth, Quivira continued. "Of course, you need not be a father to know how important it is that you tell me where my son is being held."

Rafe's fit of fury evaporated as quickly as it'd come. "Your son?" he managed to say.

"You make it sound like a question," Quivira commented, his voice turning to a snarl. "A warning, my friend, do not play games with me. Not when it comes to my son. This exchange of information takes place before dawn, or you and your friends will pay."

Hell.

But it was more than just *hell*. Rafe had plenty of blank spots, but Quivira's son wasn't one of them.

The images of battle went through Rafe's head. Specifically, the image of Colonel Shaw shooting the young man. And of him lying dead on the path. Judas Priest! And Quivira obviously thought his son had survived that attack two months earlier.

He felt Anna's touch on his arm, but Rafe turned away from her. He had to think. He had to put the pieces of this together. But he was almost positive it would not be a pretty picture when he was done.

Question one: why didn't Quivira know that his son had died? Answer: Because someone had removed the body from the battle site. If the body had been there, Quivira would have certainly found it, and they wouldn't be having this conversation.

Question two: who had removed the body? Answer: probably the same person who led Quivira to believe that Rafe knew the whereabouts of his son.

No, Rafe didn't like the way this picture was shaping up at all.

"You never did say who told you that I knew about your son." And Rafe braced himself for Quivira's answer.

"Didn't I?" Quivira paused. One second. Then, two. "The leader of your Alpha Team, of course. Colonel Ethan Shaw."

STUNNED, ANNA LISTENED as Rafe repeated the name of the person who had set this dangerous game in motion.

"I can't believe it," she said. "Why would Colonel Shaw do something like this?"

Rafe shook his head. "I don't know. Maybe it was the only way he thought he could keep the other hostages and me alive."

Maybe. But she didn't think Rafe believed that any more than she did. There were other things mixed with all of this. Things she obviously didn't know about that had placed Rafe, their baby and her in danger.

He led her to the sofa, where they sat side by side. "What I tell you can't go any further than here."

She nodded and tried to brace herself for what she might hear. Hard though to brace herself for what would likely be the details of why someone wanted them dead.

"Luke Buchanan and I were supposed to get together with O'Reilly and Quivira in separate meetings," Rafe started. "It was a setup. They thought we had a new strain of flu virus called Shadow Warrior and its antidote. We told them that we'd sell it to the highest bidder. It was actually a ploy to draw them out of hiding—something we'd been trying to do for months—so we'd stop the rebels from kidnapping any more American businessmen."

"What went wrong?" she asked.

"Everything. First of all, the Shadow Warrior virus really did go missing from the Sen-tron research facility, so Sen-tron alerted their own operative, Eve DeCalley, to track us down. That gave away our position. Then O'Reilly's troops ambushed a convoy of relief workers. Shaw split the team and sent half to try to retrieve those people before O'Reilly could take them deeper into the jungle. Signals got crossed. People weren't in the right position. And Buchanan and I were caught in the middle between O'Reilly's and Quivira's men."

Anna just sat there and listened. She'd had a taste of being caught in cross fire. It was a helpless, terrifying feeling.

"Shaw had to kill Quivira's son," Rafe continued. "And then we lost Eve DeCalley. Less than a half hour later, I was captured."

''But Shaw didn't have any part of that.'' The denial didn't ring true when she heard it aloud. ''Or did he?''

Rafe shrugged. ''Who knows? It was Shaw's plan, and he was the one doling out the orders. He's also lied about Quivira's son right from the start.''

She pressed her lips together. ''I've known Ethan Shaw most of my life. He was my father's friend. It's difficult for me to accept he'd do something underhanded.''

''I know. But someone did. Someone betrayed us. I just don't want to make the mistake of trusting the wrong person.''

And there it was. Their dilemma in a nutshell. ''But who's the wrong person, Rafe. Buchanan, maybe?''

''Hard to imagine he'd betray us and his country for money, but it's happened before.''

Yes. And she could say the same for love. Maybe Janine had turned informant because she was in love with a man who happened to be on the wrong side of the law.

Rafe scratched his head. ''The woman who died, Agent Eve DeCalley, was a security specialist at Sentron along with being Sheldon's lover. If he's the one behind this, then I figure it has something to do with her death.''

''You mean revenge?'' Anna said, thinking out

loud. "But if so, then why go after us? You didn't have anything to do with her death, did you?"

"I was there. Right in the middle of it. Maybe he felt I should have done more to stop it." He groaned in frustration. "Someone who's grieving the death of a loved one might go to all lengths to get back at the person they feel is responsible."

Anna agreed. But that didn't just apply to Sheldon; it was the same for Quivira. Once he learned that the CRO team had killed his son in that raid, nothing would stop him from coming after Rafe. Nothing. So, instead of just O'Reilly and this unknown snitch in their midst, they'd have yet another rebel leader out to kill them.

Rafe slid his arm around her. "I'll do whatever it takes to protect you and the baby."

She didn't doubt it, nor did she doubt the tenacity of those men after them. The thought of that caused Anna's stomach to clench. This wasn't over. They were all still in danger.

The phone rang again, the sound echoing through the silence. Rafe swore, apparently anticipating yet more bad news. Anna prayed he was wrong.

Instead of picking up the receiver, he switched on the speaker function.

"Rafe?" Colonel Shaw said.

"What do you want?"

"Well, for starters, I don't want you to shoot me. I'm approaching the boat as we speak."

It didn't take long for Rafe to react to that. He moved Anna behind him and snatched up his gun. ''Repeat—what do you want?''

''We have to talk. Oh, and that's not a suggestion, *Captain McQuade*. That's an order. Now, open up.''

Chapter Fourteen

The hellish roller coaster ride apparently wasn't over. Just the sound of Colonel Shaw's order sent Anna's body on high alert.

God, would this never end?

Rafe didn't say anything, but because he had backed her against the wall, she could feel the tense muscles in his body. He was primed and ready to fight. Too bad that it really might come down to that.

There was a knock at the door. Just one. Followed by the terse greeting, "Open up."

It was Colonel Shaw, all right, not that she'd doubted his visit after that order. Anna didn't dare ask what they should do. Either way would be a serious gamble.

Rafe hesitated for several long moments before he reached down and opened a concealed flap door on the floor near the foot of the sofa. "Get in," he insisted.

Anna glanced down the shallow, dark hole. If it

had an opening to the outside of the boat, she couldn't see it. Still, it seemed safer than facing down a man who might want to kill them.

"But what about you?" she mouthed.

He didn't answer her. Rafe took her arm and eased her down into the narrow coffin-like space. Anna had to crouch down so that she'd fit inside.

"Just stay put," he instructed in a rough whisper. "Rico equipped this boat with an escape tunnel. It's little more than a crawl space, but if something goes wrong, then use it to get the hell out of here. Then contact Rico at this number." He grabbed a pen from the counter and scribbled some numbers on her palm.

Anna started to argue, to tell him that they should both be trying to escape, but he stopped her. "Think of the baby," Rafe warned. "You have to keep the baby safe."

It was a dirty way to win an argument. But it worked. When Shaw pounded on the exterior door and demanded again that Rafe open up, Anna willingly went into the escape hatch. Rafe pulled out a small gun from a pocket on his pants leg and handed it to her.

"Use it if you have to," he insisted.

She nodded. "Please be careful."

"I will." He touched his mouth to hers before he closed off the opening between them.

Anna held her breath as she heard him walk across the room. Gripping the metal handle of the concealed entry, she peered out through a tiny crack. She caught a glimpse of Rafe opening the door. That glimpse had her heart pounding when Colonel Shaw stepped inside.

Anna had no trouble seeing Rafe's reaction to that. He aimed his gun right at the man.

THIS WAS ONE VISIT RAFE wished he could avoid, but he'd known all along that it was inevitable. Besides, he needed this visit almost as much as Shaw probably did. There wasn't an eyelash worth of trust between them any longer, and it was time to see the look on Shaw's face when he confronted him with what he'd learned.

Shaw stayed in the doorway, the storm raging behind him. "Where's Anna?" he asked, canvassing the area inside the boat.

"She's safe," Rafe assured him.

For a moment Rafe thought the colonel might demand her whereabouts, but Shaw only motioned toward the gun that Rafe had aimed at him.

"Aim that somewhere else. Whether you believe it or not, we're on the same side."

Rafe made a sound of mild disagreement, but he turned the gun in a slightly different direction. "How did you find me?"

"I had some equipment brought into the area so we could detect any recent movement."

Of course. Rafe knew such equipment existed—

and he knew it was a matter of time before Shaw managed to use it against him. Thank God he hadn't brought in the infrared, or Shaw would have known Anna's hiding place. Hell. Maybe he did, anyway. But for some reason, Shaw wasn't playing that hand.

"I don't suppose you've considered that someone is using our own equipment to get to us?" Rafe questioned.

Shaw nodded. "We did have a problem with that, and we fixed it."

"Yeah. Right. Trust me, I'm well aware of that problem. Someone leaked—"

"It was the Justice Department," Shaw offered. "They were monitoring our message traffic but failed to secure it. That's how O'Reilly's been tracking you. But we've stopped the information leak."

Rafe wasn't about to stake his life on that, especially since they had a team member, Luke Buchanan, who worked for the Justice Department. A coincidence that it was that particular agency that was responsible for the leaks? Rafe couldn't buy that, especially since Luke had that unexplained money in his bank account.

"We've fixed the security leaks," Shaw went on. "And we've located the hostages that Quivira's holding. I've already assembled a team to go in after them. Once they're safe, Quivira will have no reason to come after you or Anna."

It sounded good. Maybe too good. There was

something a little off with that reassurance. Rafe studied the colonel's expression but couldn't quite put his finger on it. Was Shaw trying to tell him that all was not well with that plan he'd just laid out?

Maybe.

If so, Rafe didn't need anyone to tell him that. For one thing, those hostages weren't free yet. And if securing their freedom was as imminent as Shaw had just made it out to be, then he would have waited until the mission was a done deal before making this little visit. That was standard operating procedure.

So, what did this visit mean, exactly?

Rafe decided to find out. It was time to push a few mental buttons. Little ones, though. He wouldn't bring up what Quivira had told him. Yet. "What about Janine? Is she still a player in this?"

"We don't know. A couple of hours ago she lost the tag we'd put on her."

Great. But it wasn't surprising. If Janine was a bed partner of Victor O'Reilly, then he could have easily gotten her out of the country. Or just out of the way. Rafe didn't intend to let O'Reilly do the same to Anna.

"So, here's the plan," Shaw ordered. "We get out of here right now. And by *we,* I mean all of us, including Anna. I know she's in here with you somewhere. I'm putting the two of you in protective custody until I get news back from the rescue team."

Rafe didn't respond to that. It was an order he didn't intend to obey.

"Quivira called a little while ago" was all Rafe said. "We talked."

It was enough. He could tell by the way Shaw's jaw muscles twitched that he fully understood what Quivira had divulged. The display of emotion didn't last long, though. Shaw quickly regained his military bearing.

"Did you tell him the truth about his son's death?" Shaw asked.

"No."

Shaw's poker face never faltered. No relief. No other emotion. It was the combat-rescue face that Rafe had seen dozens of times. Too bad. It was a hard face to read, and Rafe wanted to know if this man had betrayed him.

"I had my reasons for lying to Quivira," Shaw finally admitted.

Not exactly the huge confession Rafe had wanted. It wasn't nearly enough.

"And what would those reasons be?" Rafe demanded.

"Your life. Anna's. And even the lives of those other men that Quivira's holding. If Quivira knew his son was dead, then I wouldn't have anything to bargain with."

Rafe lifted a shoulder. "You know, you've lied so much that I'm not sure I want to believe that."

''What other reason would I have?''

Rafe could think of one. A bad one. Maybe Shaw had sold out his country and the members of the Alpha Team. And maybe it had something to do with that missing Shadow Warrior virus and antidote. Or all of this could be some elaborate plan to cover up an obviously botched mission. Rafe's silence let the colonel know what he was thinking.

''Quivira is the enemy,'' Shaw enunciated. ''Not me. So, make your choice now, Rafe. Either you're with me, or you're against me. Either you and Anna cooperate with this protective custody, or I'll have you both placed under arrest.''

It was the corner Rafe had expected to be boxed into. So, he went into evade-and-escape mode. As far as he was concerned, Shaw was the enemy until he could convince him otherwise, and Rafe had every intention of getting the hell out of there.

''And you think Anna and I will actually be safe in this protective custody?'' Rafe questioned.

''I'll do my best. I'll take you to the CRO training facility near San Antonio. We can regroup and wait for information about the rescue of the hostages. If necessary, we can assemble a team to take out O'Reilly and Quivira before they do any more damage. It's time for action, Rafe. I don't want to play by these goons' rules anymore.''

Yeah, and all of this *time for action* garbage could include leading the rebels right to them. It didn't matter whose side Shaw was on. Not really. It was obvious that there were holes a mile wide in security.

"Buchanan and Sheldon won't be coming with us to the training facility," Shaw promised. "I'll divert Buchanan to another project. Sheldon's already on his way back to Sen-tron headquarters for reassignment."

Surprised, Rafe just stared at him. It was a start, but it was too little too late. "If you don't trust them, then why did you leave them on the team as long as you did?"

"I thought it'd be safer until I could make other arrangements. The fewer people who knew about this, the better."

It wasn't exactly reassuring, but nothing would have been if it came from Shaw. "So, is all of this really some kind of trap, and Anna and I are the bait?"

"You've been the bait since day one," Shaw said without hesitation. "And you know it. But now it's time to minimize the threat to both of you. Yes, Quivira and O'Reilly might come after you, but they'll do it on our terms. If you're at the training facility, we can better contain them. The first step is for you to get off this boat and come with me."

Rafe would—when they started serving ice water in hell.

Shaw checked his watch. "We'll have to leave now."

"Anna's in the bathroom," Rafe said. "Give us a couple of minutes so she can get dressed, and then we can leave."

The stony look that Shaw sent him was a warning. "Don't try anything stupid. I'll be watching the boat."

Good. Maybe Shaw could keep Quivira's and O'Reilly's men at bay until he got Anna out of there.

"I'll keep this," Shaw said, taking Rafe's gun.

Rafe didn't argue. It was best not to alert Shaw to the fact that he had escape plans on his mind.

"You've got two minutes," Shaw added. And with Rafe's gun gripped in his hand, he stepped outside to wait.

RAFE DIDN'T SAY A WORD when he threw open the hatch and climbed into the cramped space with her. Anna had heard the part about "two minutes." Not much time for an escape, but Rafe obviously thought they had a chance. Or else it was a chance he had to take because it was their only option.

He took the gun from her and shoved it into his pants pocket while he maneuvered himself into a narrow tunnel that fed off the hiding space. Rafe threw back the latch.

"We'll have to do this without life jackets," he whispered, apology in his voice. "I don't want anyone to spot us. Think you can swim to shore?"

Anna nodded. She would do whatever it took to

get them out of there, but she knew her own limitations. She wasn't that strong a swimmer. "But won't Colonel Shaw be looking for us in the water?"

"Definitely."

That sent her heart pounding. She didn't have time to try to steady it. Rafe opened the small circular door, and without so much as a warning, he slid them both into the dark, cold water. The hatch door snapped shut behind them.

Overhead, the storm pounded the lake, and darkness was all around them. Rafe pulled her under the water. With his arm around her waist, he began to swim with her in tow.

It seemed several minutes, and Anna's lungs began to ache from the exertion and lack of air. Just when she thought she might panic, he surfaced. For a moment. Only long enough for her to pull in a deep breath. And then he submerged them again.

She didn't even try to look back at the boat to see if Shaw had spotted them. She kept her focus only on Rafe. Somehow, he would get them out of there.

When he neared the shore, he kept them low, in a crouch, and they crawled onto the muddy embankment. Her clothes and shoes were heavy, but Rafe didn't stop. He headed straight for a cluster of cedars and took her with him.

Panting, she heard her own ragged breath above the howl of the storm. "What now?" she asked.

He motioned toward an all-terrain vehicle that was parked near the dock. "We'll borrow that."

It probably belonged to Colonel Shaw, since it hadn't been there when they first arrived at the lake.

"Ready?" Rafe asked.

She took several deep breaths and nodded. Rafe didn't waste even a moment. He latched on to her hand and made a run for it. The night and the storm gave them some cover, but Anna had no idea if it was enough. If Shaw saw them, God knows what he would do to stop them. Maybe he would even shoot at them.

The distance between them and the vehicle seemed to widen with each step, but Rafe didn't let her slow down. Trudging through the mud and slush, he made it to the vehicle, yanked open the door and shoved her inside.

"No keys," she mumbled, looking at the ignition.

That didn't deter Rafe. He reached beneath the dash and hot-wired it.

He had only driven a few yards when she heard the sound behind them. A whirl like a rocket. Or an artillery shell. She glanced back and saw Colonel Shaw dive into the water. A split second later, she understood why. The boat exploded into a thundering ball of flames.

"Did you set explosives?" she asked, already knowing the answer.

"No."

Rafe gunned the engine and got them out of there.

Chapter Fifteen

Rafe was right. The training facility was the last place on earth anyone would have expected them to go. So, why didn't that make her feel better? Maybe it was too much to ask to feel safer simply because they'd moved to a new location.

While Rafe used the computer to check the security system, Anna opened the second-story window and looked out at the nearly deserted facility. It was midnight, and with the storm still raging, it was pitch-black outside. Only the occasional slash of lightning allowed her to see the place where the CROs and security operatives conducted some of their training.

A zigzagging obstacle course. A canine compound complete with at least a half dozen dogs. A winding hedge maze right in the center of the grounds.

In the distance, she could see a portion of a mock village and the security police checkpoint at the entrance of the facility. It was manned with two guards,

Rafe had told her, and that's why he'd carefully avoided it when he sneaked them inside an hour earlier. Instead, he had cut his way through a back fence after temporarily disarming a series of perimeter security monitors.

Anna glanced over her shoulder when she heard Rafe walk toward her. The room was functional and little else. An office, of sorts, jammed with computers and other equipment. Earlier, Rafe had changed into his uniform and put several small pieces of that equipment into a black duffel bag. Preparing for his mission, no doubt. A mission that was inevitable. Dangerous. And necessary.

"Quivira refused to do any negotiations over the phone," he told her. "That's what I figured he'd say, so I've set up a meeting with him at his choice of locations. The cabin we were shot at. I'll give him the information about his son and tell him, if possible, I'll arrange to have the body returned to him. Hopefully, that'll start the ball rolling for a cease-fire."

What Rafe left unsaid was that the meeting was only a part of what he had to do. He couldn't let Quivira go free. That was the real reason the meeting had to be face-to-face. The man was a killer, and as long as he was out there, their lives and others would always be in danger. Rafe would have to put an end to that threat even if it meant eliminating Quivira.

The thought of Rafe facing Quivira made Anna

ache. After all, Quivira was about to learn his son was dead. God knows how he would react to news like that. A cease-fire and return of his son's body might be the last things on his mind. He might come at Rafe with guns blazing.

Of course, Rafe knew that as well as she did.

"What about Victor O'Reilly?" Anna asked. "He wants to kill us, too, and in some ways he's more dangerous than Quivira since he doesn't want to trade any information."

"Rico is going after him. He's already back in the States and on the way to a bravo location where he's arranged to intercept O'Reilly. It's an abandoned house about six miles from the cabin where I'm meeting Quivira. Rico had to blow his undercover identity to find out the man's location, but I couldn't risk having O'Reilly out there any longer."

He was right, of course. "And what about Colonel Shaw? Does he know about this?"

"No. I didn't let Shaw, Buchanan or Sheldon in on our plan. Too risky," Rafe added. "Anyway, Shaw's tied up with the hostage rescue. It should all be over by morning."

He sounded calm. Comforting. Even confident. But it was partly a facade, and they both knew it. Nothing had gone right so far. Well, nothing except for the fact they were still somehow miraculously alive. But that had more to do with Rafe's tenacity than it did anything else.

"I have to stop all of this," Rafe continued as if trying to convince her that there was no other way. Which there probably wasn't. "And I can't take you with me. It's too dangerous. You'll be safe here."

Maybe.

Anna kept that thought to herself. She would certainly be safer at the training compound than she would at that cabin with Quivira and God knows who else. But then, if Rafe had broken through security to get inside the facility, then others could as well.

Anna pushed that thought aside, too.

Rafe stepped closer, until his chest was against her back. He brushed a kiss on her cheek and slid his arms around her. Even after that swim through the lake and the trek through the surrounding woods, he smelled good. Musky and warm.

"You'll be all right," he assured her. "I'll do whatever it takes to protect you."

It wasn't the first time he'd promised that, and there was no sense of *maybe* in it. Anna had doubts about how all of these meetings and the rescue mission would end, but her worries had nothing to do with Rafe's abilities. If it could be done, then he would do it.

She wrapped her arms around his and tightened the grip. "When do you leave?"

"In less than two hours. I have to wait until the task force has gotten the hostages out."

Not much time, considering it could possibly be

the last time she would ever see him. But Anna had no intentions of voicing that. She had less than one hundred and twenty minutes to spend with the man she loved, and she didn't intend to waste it with fears and regrets.

"I'm very good at what I do," he whispered. "And I've got a heck of a lot of reasons to finish off this mess and come back to you." He placed his hand on her stomach. "This is just one of them."

Anna smiled in spite of everything. Earlier, she had thought he didn't even want the baby. Thankfully, she'd been wrong.

She could have pushed the moment. And almost did. It would have been wonderful to hear Rafe say that he loved her, but it would have been a lie. Or at least a half truth. He still didn't remember the love he'd once felt for her. And might never remember.

Could she accept that?

It didn't take Anna more than a few seconds to realize the answer. To be with Rafe, she could accept just about anything except losing him.

She turned toward him, sliding her arms around his neck in the same motion. It was the need for reassurance that sent her in search of his mouth. But it was the love she felt for him that made her deepen the kiss.

The taste of him jolted through her. It soothed her. Nourished her. Made her feel as if everything was right with the world. She forgot about the rebels who were after them, the storm, and the mission that still lay ahead. She was safe now and right where she belonged.

His response was instant. A burst of energy. A kiss that matched the need in her. And not exactly meant for reassurance. It was laced with hunger and fire.

For days, they'd been testing and resisting this need they had for each other. Rafe had even managed to show her a thing or two about how he could pleasure her. But they'd yet to make love.

It was time to do something about that.

Anna released her grip on him so she could get closer. Rafe did the same. Until they were pressed against each other. They tried to satisfy the fire with their mouths. With their hurried caresses. With the contact of their bodies. But it wasn't enough.

Not nearly enough.

Anna struggled to hold on to her breath even though she wasn't sure she wanted to breathe just yet. The light-headed giddiness felt like a swirl of magic that had snared her in a sensual web. But she knew the source of the magic was really Rafe.

He backed her against the wall. It was a good thing, or she would have certainly lost her balance. She tugged with the buttons on his battle-dress uniform. And won. She finally managed to get off his shirt so she could put her hands on his naked chest.

Mercy, the man was built.

All those tight rippled muscles. The rough coils of

chest hair. The sinewy feel of all that power and strength beneath her hands. His body was a honed lethal weapon, and yet she'd never felt more cherished than she did when those strong arms held her.

"I know this isn't the best time or the best place," she whispered.

"Yeah. We've had a little trouble with that right place, right time thing, haven't we?" He peeled off her oversize T-shirt and tossed it aside. "First that cellar in Monte de Leon. Then the boat. And now this office where there's not a freaking bed in sight."

"We don't need a bed."

He chuckled in that low, sexy way that only Rafe could manage. "My thoughts, exactly. We'll just have to make our own bed…and then lie down in it."

It was exactly what she wanted. *This* was what she wanted. And no, it might not have been the right time or the right place, but this was definitely the right man.

The only man.

Anna went exploring. They didn't have a lot of time, but she didn't intend to skip any of the pleasures along the way. She caressed those taut muscles of his chest and gently circled his nipple with her fingertips. She got her reward when he groaned with pleasure.

Rafe did his own share of exploring. He matched her almost-frantic pace with his hurried kisses and touches. He tugged at her jeans, the snap finally giving way so that he could slide them off her. On his way back up, he planted some kisses on her thighs and stomach.

His movements slowed when he reached her panties. He was gentle. No heated rush even though the clock was ticking. Anna pushed the thought of that clock aside. And everything else. Instead, she concentrated on the kisses. The touches. And Rafe.

"I probably should have said this sooner, but should we be doing this?" he asked. He eased away from her slightly and caught her gaze.

He meant because she was pregnant. "Definitely. The doctor said it was okay."

And Anna pulled him back to her.

Tired of the barriers between them, she rid him of the rest of his uniform, and with the wall still supporting them, they slid down to the floor. Anna took advantage of the new position. Face to face, mouth to mouth, chest to chest, body to body. She eased onto his lap and wrapped her legs around his waist.

"Let's do this now." Anna rubbed herself against his erection, hoping to take him inside her right then and there.

But Rafe obviously had other plans.

He dodged her maneuvers and dropped a line of kisses from her mouth to her breasts. "You're so beautiful."

They were words of seduction, but they weren't

necessary. The seduction had not only been mutual but was very near completion. But in her heart, Anna knew she would remember that compliment for the rest of her life.

She said his name. As a plea. And as a promise. His body slid against hers. Damp bare skin against bare skin. His breath brushed over her face.

"Anna," he whispered.

Just the sound of Rafe saying her name was enough to send the fire roaring through her blood. "Make love to me," she insisted.

"Soon."

Rafe fisted his hands in her hair and forced her head back so that he could take her neck. Nothing was slow about this pace. Nothing gentle. He took. And claimed. And savored.

It still wasn't enough.

"More," she insisted.

Rafe flashed her one of those dazzling grins. "More was exactly what I had in mind."

RAFE KNEW THIS HAD ALREADY reached the point of no return. *More,* Anna had requested. And that's exactly what he would give her.

"Hang on, darling," he said. "What do you say we go on this ride together?"

She made a soft, shivery sound. Part laughter, part invitation. All need.

Rafe captured her gaze and entered her slowly. Gently. Enjoying every inch of the delicate resistance that he met. Until he was fully inside her.

A few coherent thoughts crossed his mind, but none were exactly the romantic declarations he was looking for. So, Rafe tried a simpler approach.

"This is right," he managed to say.

She nodded, her breath coming out in gentle gusts. "You bet it is."

He stilled another moment. To catch his breath. To absorb the incredible feel of her. Her silky heat pulsed around him. But that heat and warmth that he saw in Anna's eyes put a quick end to that moment of stillness.

Rafe had no choice. He began to move inside her. Need dictated the pace and the intensity. And there was so much need in both of them.

As if his life depended on it, he drove into her. She accepted him, moved with him.

She whispered his name, repeated it, a trembling sound spilling over her lips. He plummeted them both, too quickly, he thought, to that ultimate moment. Any amount of time would have been too little. Too fast. For something he wanted to last forever.

He would tell her that later. Later, when words mattered.

For now, he gathered her beneath him, until all she could do was cling to him to save her.

And he did.

Following her, Rafe did his best to save them both.

WITH HER WRAPPED IN his arms, Rafe let his mind drift. He tried to absorb the enormity of his relationship with Anna, their feelings for each other and everything else.

The night settled in around them. The dark room. Anna's scent on his skin. The gentle rhythm of her heartbeat against his hand. The sound of the storm outside.

And then it happened.

The memories came like video clips. Short bursts of sights, sounds, smells, tastes and touches. Images of Anna. Of the rescue in Monte de Leon. Of that cellar where he'd made love to her.

Everything.

Little by little, it all came back. The small details that were more valuable, more treasured than any tangible possession could ever have been. The first time he'd kissed Anna. The taste of her. The way she'd fit in his arms. And the love. God, the love. It was there. Strong and real. A place in his heart meant only for her.

All of the missing pieces of the past twelve months of his life came back to him.

Rafe caught on to each one. Reliving them. Cherishing them. The pain and the happiness. Most of all the happiness. Before Anna, he hadn't even known what that word truly meant.

Now, he did.

And he would do whatever it took to hold on to that. To hold on to her and their child.

Rafe savored the images and feelings a moment longer before pushing them aside. He couldn't let any of that distract him now.

He kissed her and moved away from her.

"It's time?" she asked.

He nodded, reaching for his clothes. Anna got up also, and they dressed in silence. After he'd donned his battle dress uniform, he put a phone and a handgun on the table near her. He prayed she didn't need either, but they might come in handy if security failed.

Or if *he* failed.

"You'll be careful?" There was a catch in her voice, but she quickly cleared her throat to try to cover it. She was obviously trying to be strong for him.

"Absolutely." And because he wanted to see that dazzling smile, Rafe looped an arm around her waist and snapped her to him. "Don't worry. All this top-secret kind of stuff is right up my alley, darling. I'll be back before breakfast."

It didn't work. Anna tried to force a smile, but instead her mouth quivered. "Just don't take any unnecessary chances, all right?"

"No plans for that," he assured her. "This will be a quick in and out. Promise. Then Quivira won't be able to get to us anymore."

From his mouth to God's receptive ears. More

than anything he wanted to make it back to Anna and their child, and it just might take some help of a divine nature.

"I hate to ask," she started, her voice still low and shaky. "But you do trust Rico, don't you?"

"Of course. I've known him for years."

She lifted a shoulder. "I could say the same about Colonel Shaw. I just don't want you to let friendship blind you to things that might not be right."

It was no easy request. Rico had saved his life not once but twice. That created trust on the deepest level possible. Still, Anna was right. These were not ordinary times. Someone with plenty of insider knowledge had been helping both sides of the rebels. That didn't mean he wouldn't trust Rico to help him with this mission. But he planned to do a lot of looking over his shoulder.

Rafe planted a kiss on her forehead and forced himself away from her so he could finish packing his equipment bag. "Lock the door when I go, and don't leave this room. I'll make sure the security system is set. Plus, there are guards at the gate. Press that red button by the door if you need them."

Anna nodded. And paused. Her eyes slowly lifted to meet his. "What is it?" she asked. "Is something wrong that I don't know about?"

"Everything's fine," he assured her.

It was another of those not-so-little white lies that

he'd been doling out lately. He wouldn't tell her that he'd regained his memory. Not now. Not while he was on his way out the door. There wasn't enough time to work through all the implications and conversations of something like that. Later, when he returned, he'd tell her. Later, he would make everything all right.

But first, he had to face down the devil and somehow survive it.

Chapter Sixteen

Rafe had a bad feeling about this. Real bad.

He stayed crouched in the shallow crevice on the limestone bluff and gave his infrared equipment another adjustment. He scanned the cabin. The woods. And even the road. Again. He repeated the procedure to make sure the monitor was working correctly.

It was.

So, why hadn't he gotten a reading to indicate that someone, anyone, was nearby?

Quivira had promised to come alone, but Rafe had automatically dismissed that as a bald-faced lie. He'd come prepared to battle it out with at least a dozen armed men who would try to capture him. Instead, Rafe found himself alone in the woods.

"Status?" he heard Rico ask through the earpiece communicator.

"Too quiet. How about you?"

"The same. The house looks empty. O'Reilly's a no-show."

Definitely not good. So, what the hell was going on?

"Have the SkyWatch pilot do an aerial read," Rafe instructed Rico.

Not that Rafe would trust such an aerial read over the equipment he had in his hands, but it seemed time to get a second opinion.

While he waited for the data, and while the silence lay heavy around him, Rafe couldn't help but think of Anna. Maybe Murphy's Law wouldn't play havoc with them again, and maybe she'd stay safe until he could finish this mission and get back to her.

He was in love with her. No doubt about it. And he hadn't needed the return of his memory to tell him that. Somewhere along the way, in the middle of the chaos, he'd fallen in love with her all over again. There was something comforting about that. No matter what they faced, no matter what the challenges, the love he felt for Anna would always be a constant.

His true north.

And he couldn't get any better anchor than that. Now all he had to do was rid the world of Quivira and make his way back to her.

Rafe heard a slight crackle of static in his ear. "Nothing from the aerial report," Rico relayed to him. "There's been some recent activity, but none in the last hour. This isn't looking good, Rafe."

No, it wasn't.

He considered his options, but there was really only one choice. He had to check out the cabin, to see if Quivira had left a note about a secondary meeting place. Of course, if the man had done that, it would essentially mess up everything. Rafe would lose the advantage of position and territory. And it would mean wasting time here when he should be making his way back to Anna.

But what choice did he have?

"I'm going in," Rafe mumbled.

"You sure about that?" Rico asked.

"No. But I'm doing it anyway."

"Then I guess I will, too. If O'Reilly's in the house, I'll find him. Good luck. Don't break a leg or anything."

"Same to you," Rafe offered.

He took a deep breath, said a quick prayer and climbed out of the crevice. When he got to the top, he stayed in a crouched position and began to make his way down the rough terrain toward the cabin.

The rain had stopped nearly an hour earlier, but the ground was slick with mud. Rafe adjusted the equipment on his back and wormed his way though the mat of shrubs and cedars.

There were no lights on in the cabin, and the dark-colored logs seemed to blend into the moonless night. He glanced at the infrared motion detector to make sure no one had circled around behind him, but he seemed to have the place to himself.

So, why didn't that make him feel better?

He took another reading as he reached the back porch, but when that was negative as well, he put the equipment away and slipped inside.

Rafe paused a moment. Listening. He heard nothing. Not even a whisper of breath. That bad feeling in his gut went up a considerable notch. He went through the kitchen, gingerly stepping over broken glass from Quivira's earlier attack. He moved without a sound, keeping his weapon ready in case he had to fire.

His eyes had already adjusted to the darkness by the time he made it to the living room, so he had no trouble seeing the man in the chair near the fireplace. But not just any man.

Quivira.

"Oh, hell," Rafe muttered.

He went closer, knowing what he would find. Still, he pressed his fingers to the man's neck.

No pulse.

No body heat.

Nothing.

Not only was Quivira dead, he'd been that way for some time. Hours, at least. And that meant the whole meeting had probably been a setup.

"Good news and bad news," he heard Rico say into the earpiece. "The hostages are free. But O'Reilly's already a goner. Not my handiwork, either. He was dead when I arrived."

''Quivira, too.''

Both men cursed at the same time.

Rafe hurried out of the cabin, praying he was wrong. He'd never forgive himself if Quivira and O'Reilly's killer had already gone after Anna. But in his heart, he knew that's exactly what had happened.

ANNA FOUND HERSELF on her knees in front of the toilet. Talk about a bad time for her first bout with morning sickness. She pressed the wad of wet paper towels to her forehead, hoping it would help. It did, some, but there was still a heavy, queasy feeling in the pit of her stomach.

There was a security light just outside the bathroom window. Just enough so she could catch sight of herself in the full-length mirror mounted on the wall. She had the paper towels in one hand. The gun in the other. Her face was colorless. And she was still rumpled—the remnants of making love with Rafe.

Talk about a visual summary of her predicament.

The only thing missing was a huge sign around her neck saying how worried she was about him. He had to be all right. She wouldn't let herself consider anything else.

The sound of the phone ringing cut through the dull ache in her head, and she got to her feet and raced into the adjoining room to answer it.

''Please let it be Rafe,'' she mumbled.

But it wasn't Rafe at all.

"Anna?" Janine said.

Stunned, Anna took a moment to gather her breath. "How did you get this number?"

"Colonel Shaw patched me through. We have to talk, Anna. Now."

Mercy. She didn't need this. She already had enough to deal with.

"This isn't a good time, Janine." Anna went to the window and since the glass was coated with condensation, she opened it and checked the grounds. She didn't see anyone, but Janine's call made her very uneasy. If Shaw could patch her through, what else could he do? Could he find her? And if he could, what would he do with that information? "I need to keep this line open in case Rafe calls."

"This is important. Just listen. Someone used me to get to you and Rafe."

Anna's throat constricted. God, it was true. She'd hoped that Shaw and the others had been wrong, that Janine didn't have any part in this. But it appeared that she was the one who was wrong.

"I know about your friendship with Victor O'Reilly," Anna challenged.

"Friendship? Not quite. That would imply a two-way street. He's a user, Anna, and I hadn't heard from him in years until just about a week ago. I had no idea—none—as to what he planned to do, but I think he had someone put something in your wedding ring. A microchip tracking device or something. And I think he's been using it to find you.''

Anna's gaze flew to the chunky emerald-cut diamond wedding band. The ring that Janine had no doubt helped Rafe buy from her own jewelry store.

''Get rid of it now,'' Janine insisted. ''Someone had broken into the jewelry store. I think now it was someone who worked for O'Reilly. He didn't take anything so I thought it was kids. I didn't put it together until I talked to Colonel Shaw and he asked if there was any personal item of yours that O'Reilly might have had access to.''

''You think he had access to my ring?'' Anna asked.

''He had access to the whole damn store. He could have put that tracking chip in the setting before the wedding. I'm so sorry, Anna. I swear I didn't know.''

The blood rushed to her head and sent the room spinning. Anna fought it and forced herself to stay focused. She laid the gun aside, cradled the phone against her ear and tugged at the ring.

It wouldn't budge.

God, it wouldn't budge! The only thought going through her head was that O'Reilly or one of his henchmen was already on his way to kill her.

Frantic, Anna ran to the bathroom and stuck her hand under the running water. The ring finally slipped off. She wasted no time. Anna flushed it down the toilet.

"I got it off," she told Janine.

Anna didn't think the sigh she heard from her friend was fake, and it matched her own.

The relief didn't last long.

"O'Reilly could have already tracked you," Janine pointed out. "Can you go somewhere else—fast?"

"Rafe told me to stay here until he got back."

But the moment she said the words, Anna regretted it. She'd just perhaps told the enemy that she was alone. And vulnerable. Worse, the line went dead.

She pressed the flash button, hoping to reconnect with Janine, but all she got was silence. Silence, until she heard the click. The soft sound came from the lock.

The door opened slowly.

"Good evening, Anna," the person greeted. "I thought I might find you here."

Chapter Seventeen

Anna heard the all-too-familiar voice, and it made her blood run cold. It wasn't Buchanan. Or Shaw. Or even Janine. Nicholas Sheldon was in the doorway of the room.

Every inch of Anna's body went on alert. God, how had he gotten so close without her even hearing him?

"Sheldon. You scared the life out of me." She pressed her hand over her heart. It was too late not to jump to conclusions. She'd already jumped but prayed she was wrong. "What are you doing here?"

Without so much as a word, Sheldon stepped inside and closed the door behind him.

Just that simple gesture made Anna want to take a step back, but she forced herself to hold her ground. She didn't know why, but she didn't intend to let Sheldon know just how much she was afraid of him. "I'll have to ask you to leave. Rafe will be back soon."

"I won't stay long." He leaned against the door, almost casually, and stared at her.

Anna suddenly didn't care if he heard the fear in her voice. "There's nothing we have to say to each other."

"Yes." He paused. "There is."

Somehow, Anna knew what was about to happen. She'd known from the moment she saw him in the doorway. Running from the rebels had honed her survival instincts, and those instincts were screaming for her to get out of there.

She whipped her gaze to the desk. The gun Rafe had left her was still there. Just out of reach. With Sheldon's strength and speed, he could easily overpower her even before she could get to it.

And he would overpower her.

Anna was sure of that.

"You used the tracking device in the ring to find me," she said more to herself than him. She glanced at the emergency button by the door. Sheldon was between it and her.

"No. That was O'Reilly's doing, I guess. I used Sen-tron's equipment that the Justice Department paid for."

He walked closer, still blocking her path to the emergency button. "This has to be quick." His words were calm. Void of any emotion. He could have been discussing the weather instead of his plans to kill her. "Did I mention these rooms are virtually soundproof? One of Colonel Shaw's idiosyncrasies. He tolerates no information leaks during training. Ironic, isn't it?''

So, no one would hear her if she screamed. Anna fought to keep control of her breath. Her composure. If she panicked, she stood no chance against a man like Sheldon. She had to keep her wits so she could figure out what to do.

He pulled something from inside his shirt. Something wrapped in a washcloth. With his back still braced against the wall, he carefully unwrapped it, and Anna noticed then that he wore surgical gloves. She didn't have long to dwell on that because cradled in the cloth was a gun fitted with a silencer. She couldn't be sure, but it appeared to be the gun Colonel Shaw had carried that night at the church.

God, was Sheldon trying to set this up to make it seem as if Shaw had killed her?

''Rafe could come walking in here at any moment,'' she warned.

''No. He won't. He's still very much tied up with his meeting with Quivira. He probably won't figure out that Quivira is dead for…oh, at least another half hour or so.''

Dead. Quivira was dead. Not that it would help her now. Had the meeting with Rafe and Quivira been just a ruse? Probably. If so, it was an effective one.

She'd be dead if she didn't do something to save

herself. And she would do something. But what? There didn't seem any place to run or hide.

"You're doing this because of that woman who died on a CRO rescue mission?" But it wasn't really a question. Anna just wanted to keep him talking until she could figure out what to do.

"Yes," he readily answered. He winced as if just admitting that was painful. "Eve DeCalley. I was in love with her. An emotion that I'm sure you understand completely. Imagine how heartbroken you'd be if you lost Rafe. Eve's dead because of your husband and Colonel Shaw. Their incompetence killed her. She would have never been caught in that cross fire if it weren't for them."

Anna shook her head and gathered enough breath to speak. "That's not the way I heard it."

"Then you heard it wrong," he calmly assured her. There was a twisted sort of triumph in his voice. "I've already taken care of Quivira and O'Reilly. Dregs of society. You're next, my dear. And then your husband, of course."

"What about Shaw?"

"I'll save the best for last. His won't be nearly as quick and painless. He'll be court-martialed and eventually put to death for killing Rafe and you to cover up his botched mission."

With each word, Anna fought off the despair. She wouldn't let this man win.

Sheldon stuffed the washcloth back in his shirt and

raised the gun. Anna did back up then. Just a step. Out of the corner of her eye, she saw the window— the window she'd opened earlier.

He angled his gaze in that direction as well. It was a contingency he probably hadn't counted on. The room might be soundproof, but with an open window, perhaps one of the security policemen would hear her scream.

Now, if she could get close enough for the sound to carry.

"I wouldn't do that if I were you," he warned.

"But you're not me, are you?" she fired back.

A brief smile bent his mouth.

And he took aim.

There was no time to decide what to do—Anna dove onto the side of the table away from him. The shot, hardly more than a swish of air, slammed into the wall above her head and sent a chunk of plaster flying. She didn't stop. She didn't take the time to think about how close Sheldon had just come to killing her.

She yelled, praying the security policemen at the gate would hear her and respond. But she couldn't wait to see if that would happen. She yanked some papers off one of the desks, flung them at Sheldon and, in the same motion, scrambled across the room to try to get to her gun.

Sheldon beat her to it.

He swiped the weapon off the table and threw it

well out of her reach. With their bodies only inches apart, their gazes collided. For a moment. And then he sprang toward her. He might have been bigger, but Anna somehow managed to dodge his grip. She hurried around the end of the table and headed straight for the window.

Another shot slammed into the wall next to her shoulder, missing her only because she ducked at the last possible second. It didn't stop her. Nothing would at this point. If she stayed in the room, she'd die.

Anna cried out for help again. She barreled onto the windowsill and climbed out onto the ledge that lipped the building. It wasn't a large space by any means. Mere inches. There was no place for her to hide, so she needed a temporary barricade until she could find a way out.

"It won't do any good to yell," Sheldon told her as he walked closer. "I took care of the sky cops at the gate. You don't think I'd let them interfere with my plans, do you?"

Oh, God. He'd killed them. Not that she had any doubts, but that meant he wouldn't hesitate to kill her.

She slammed the window shut just as the glass shattered from another bullet. Fortunately, the glass was covered with a safety coating so the shards merely cracked and webbed. If it hadn't, she would have almost certainly been cut.

"You're like a cat with nine lives," Sheldon grumbled. "But those lives have already been used up."

Anna screamed again, praying that someone, anyone, would hear her, but she didn't intend to wait around and see. Crouching, she caught sight of the ground below.

"Oh, God," she gasped.

The ledge was probably less than ten feet high, but it suddenly seemed miles away. The jump would perhaps injure her. Or worse, it might hurt the baby, especially if Sheldon could shoot again before she could take cover. But she didn't have a choice. When she heard the sound of him walking toward her, Anna said a prayer.

And jumped.

The scream that tore from her mouth wasn't calculated this time or meant to alert anyone. It was from pain when she hit the ground and twisted her ankle. Anna ignored it. Or tried to and scrambled into a bed of sage bushes. Any moment, Sheldon would come out onto the ledge and shoot at her. If she stayed put, she'd be an easy target.

On all fours, she scurried behind a clumpy hedge and peered up at the window. She cringed when she saw Sheldon already there. His gun, already aimed. Right at her.

Keeping low, she managed to stand, wincing at the

almost unbearable pain in her ankle, and darted behind another hedge.

A shot blistered through the air overhead.

She ran and called out for help again. Panic and fear raced through her, nearly choking off her breath. She fought for each bit of air that she managed to pull into her lungs. But she didn't stop. Anna knew she had to put some distance, some space, between Sheldon and her. She had to take cover.

But where?

Still running, she spotted the maze just ahead. Not her first choice of hiding places, but the hedges were thick and high. Maybe Sheldon wouldn't be able to see her from the balcony. That wouldn't stop him from pursuing her, of course, but this way, she at least had a fighting chance.

"Please," she prayed, racing through the entrance of the maze. "Don't let him hurt the baby."

The path between the hedge rows was narrow, probably not even enough room for two people to walk side by side. Obviously not meant for romantic strolls in the moonlight. It reminded her of a spooky carnival ride with its sharp turns and deep shadows. It was so dark, she couldn't even see the ground beneath her feet.

When her lungs ached so much that she thought they might burst, Anna stopped and caught on to one of the hedges. She rifled through the stiff branches, batting them aside. It only took her a moment to realize that she wouldn't be able to escape through the tightly knitted shrubs.

But she saw something that had her heart nearly stopping in mid-beat.

In the distance, she could see the building. And the window. Sheldon was still in it, peering out into the yard at the maze. Even through the murky darkness, she could tell that he didn't have his gun raised. Nor did he appear to be ready to come after her.

He blew into a whistle, the sound high-pitched and shrill. And then he stepped back inside.

Anna had no time to wonder why he'd done that. No time to think. She heard the dogs bark. And knew the sound hadn't come from the pen. They were closer.

Much closer.

Sheldon had sent the attack dogs after her.

THE STRANGE SOUND THAT RAFE heard had him going still just outside the building where he'd left Anna. He listened. And a moment later, he heard it again. Someone had screamed.

Not someone.

Anna.

Rafe started to bolt inside the building, but he realized the sound hadn't come from there. It was outside. Somewhere on the grounds.

Hell.

Why was she outside?

"Anna?" he called out.

Nothing.

And that caused his heart to drop to his knees.

"Anna?" he shouted even louder. Using the building for cover, he stepped around the side and glanced up at the window of the training room where she was supposed to be.

No one was there.

In the distance he heard the dogs bark. The sound went right through him. He glanced around the area, trying to figure out where the dogs were. And Anna.

"Rafe!" she yelled.

There was no doubt in his mind that she was in the maze, and when he whipped his attention in that direction, he saw the dogs race inside the narrow hedge opening.

Rafe broke into a sprint. God knows why she was there, but he had to get to her before the dogs did. They would tear her to pieces.

He whistled, hoping the dogs would respond to the training prompt. But it was a long shot. One that obviously didn't work. The dogs had been trained to respond to a whistle that the security police used. He didn't know where the cops were, but he couldn't count on them showing up to help Anna.

A shot whipped through the air, smashing into the ground just ahead of him. Rafe cursed and dove for cover. Someone was shooting at him.

But who?

It didn't take him long to come up with that answer. It was probably the person who was responsible for Anna being in that maze.

"Anna, I'm coming!" Rafe shouted.

No gunman or attack dogs would stop him. He used the hedges, running between them, darting in and out of the open yard. He had to keep the movement random. That way, the shooter wouldn't have such an easy target. Easy to say but hard to do when Anna's life was at stake.

Within seconds, he'd reached the back side of the house. Rafe never paused. He raced to a sprawling live oak. Then to another. He heard the dogs again, their incessant barking, and knew they were on Anna's trail.

There was a good twenty feet of open yard between him and the maze. Space he'd have to cover the hard way because there wasn't time to find a circuitous route.

"Rafe?" someone shouted.

Not Anna. Colonel Shaw.

That didn't do a lot to make him feel better about their situation. Rafe knew he only had seconds to react, precious seconds to figure out what to do. If he'd been wrong, if it was Shaw firing those shots, then he'd deal with that—and Shaw—later. Right now, he had to stay alive and get to Anna.

Zigzagging, Rafe darted out into the open space. The entrance to the maze suddenly seemed miles away, and he knew at any moment another bullet could come flying through the darkness. Even if he got hit, he prayed for the strength to save Anna from those dogs and from the shooter.

Rafe whistled again, trying to find the right pitch, but the dogs just kept on barking.

Several shots came at him. One right behind the other. From experience he knew these weren't from a handgun but a high-powered rifle fitted with a silencer. No silencer, however, could muffle that kind of noise, and Rafe was able to pinpoint the direction from where they came.

Inside the house.

The second floor.

And that meant someone had practically an aerial view with which to kill.

Still running, he approached the maze not from the entrance, but from the side. Rafe slid through a narrow crevice between two hedges. He'd known it was there—he'd discovered it and others during the multiple training missions at the facility. He slipped into the narrow corridor, the sharp branches gashing his uniform, and he ran toward the sound of the dogs.

If Anna had known her way around the grounds, she probably could have figured her way out of the maze. It was basically a mile-long stretch of bends, turns and circles that had a somewhat predicable pattern. But since this was probably her first time in it, Rafe had to guess which direction she might go. The dogs didn't give him any clues. Their vicious barks filled the air, choking out any other sounds.

"Anna!" Rafe shouted again.

It would probably give away his position to the shooter, but it might also get the dogs moving toward him. At a minimum, the pack might split up, and that would give Anna a better chance of survival if they attacked.

He prayed they wouldn't attack.

Over the din of the animals, Rafe thought he heard her answer. He raced through the path, willing himself to find her, but with each corridor, he came up empty.

And then he heard her scream.

A horrifying sound.

He had no doubts. Anna was battling for her life.

Chapter Eighteen

A dead end.

Damn it! She'd reached a dead end. And she was trapped. The maze pinned her in on both sides, and behind her, she could hear the sounds of the dogs approaching.

God, she didn't want to die.

Shouting out another plea for help, Anna banged her hands against the wall of hedges, knowing the gesture was futile but unable to stop herself.

And then she heard the first growl.

Not some distant sound. No. This was nearby. At least one of the dogs was very close.

Anna turned slowly toward the corridor and prayed she was wrong.

She wasn't.

Even in the darkness, she could see the shimmer of the animal's eyes.

She forced herself not to make any sudden moves. "Stop," she ordered. She even tried whistling, since that's how Sheldon had started the attack in the first place.

Anna couldn't tell if the dog obeyed her order, but she knew this one wouldn't be alone for long. She could already hear the others racing down the passageway straight toward her. When they were together as a pack, then they would no doubt attack as they'd been trained to do.

"Talk to me, Anna," Rafe called out.

His voice gave her hope and made her even more frightened. If he walked into the middle of this, he might be killed as well. She didn't want to risk that, but she didn't want to die, either.

"I need to hear you," Rafe added.

He was trying to find her. But how could he do that in the dark maze?

"The dogs are in here, too," she warned. "And I'm at a dead end."

The dog in front of her snarled even louder, and she sensed that he moved closer. Worse, she heard the others. The pants of their angry breaths. The smell of the run. They were moving in for the kill.

Anna fought the black wave of panic that washed through her. She couldn't give in to it. She rammed her hand into the hedges and cursed when she felt the metal rods that braced the trunks. The rods were only inches apart. Like the bars in a jail cell that had imprisoned her. Still, she tried to pry them from the ground.

"Rafe? Where are you?" she called again.

"Inside the maze."

Not necessarily close to her, though. Anna just couldn't tell. But even if he did manage to get to the correct corridor, there was a possibility he wouldn't be able to stop all the dogs before they attacked.

"Damn you, Sheldon," Anna mumbled. Keeping her gaze locked on the dog, she whistled and heard Rafe do the same.

She reached behind her again and tried to latch on to the hedges so she could hoist herself up. They were thick, matted together in a thorny tangle with the metal rods, but the fronds themselves simply snapped in her hands. She kept hold of one of the larger branches, hoping to use it to protect herself. It wasn't much, but it was better than nothing.

Another dog raced around the corner and into the corridor. He wasn't alone. Since her eyes had adjusted to the darkness, Anna had no trouble seeing a third. And then a fourth. They fanned out as much as they could and stalked toward her.

She backed against the hedges and kept the branch raised in front of her like a shield.

"Anna?" Rafe called out.

He was close, but she didn't dare answer him now. The dogs would almost certainly attack her if she made any sudden noise or if she tried to climb over the hedges. Of course, they'd likely do the same if she stayed perfectly quiet. Still, she wanted to buy herself as many seconds as she could.

The dog in the front of the pack growled. He moved. Not inches. He sprang forward. At the same time, the others moved as well. All lunging at her.

On a ragged scream, Anna grabbed on to the hedges to try to hoist herself up.

RAFE FELT HIS WAY ALONG the hedges and cursed the darkness. With just a few threads of light, he would have already found what he was looking for. Thank God he had at least an audible way to locate her.

Too bad the audible included her frantic, terrified screams and the sounds of the dogs as they made their way toward her. From the way the hedges rattled, she was obviously trying to climb over them.

An impossible task.

Rafe knew because he'd tried that himself. The hedges simply weren't designed to support weight. Not the weight of a person, anyway. And the bramble beneath would cut flesh to shreds.

He didn't waste time reassuring her but prayed she would hold on long enough for him to reach her. While he was at it, he added a prayer that the maze was the same as it had been since he'd first done training there. If not, then he could be in a hell of a lot of trouble.

And Anna and his baby could be dead.

But Rafe didn't intend for that to happen.

He shoved his hands through the hedges, working at a frenzied pace until he came to the spot—the slit that he'd wormed his way through to beat the designated enemy at the maze game. One of dozens of slits that the designer had included in the dead ends in case a trainee was smart enough to try some creative evade-and-escape maneuvers.

Like now.

"It's me," he shouted. "Take my hand."

"Where?"

Rafe didn't wait for her to locate it. He felt around until he latched on to her arm, and with a fierce jerk, he pulled her through.

His gun was already in position to fire, but first he shoved her behind him. He aimed the shots high, hopefully over the dogs' heads, but if he had to, he would shoot to kill. Without a silencer, the two rounds he fired exploded with a deafening blast.

He paused. Waited. And listened.

When he heard the animals running away, he knew the shots had done the trick. Now he waited to see if the gunfire had also alerted the person who wanted them dead.

He hooked his arm around Anna's waist and roughly pulled her to him. "Sheldon," she said, her breath coming out in rough, loud gasps.

"Sheldon?"

"He's the one behind this. He tried to kill me because of the woman who died on one of your missions.''

Yes. And Sheldon was no doubt the one who'd killed O'Reilly and Quivira—in retaliation for Eve's death. He'd also likely fired those shots at him. And from the sound the shots made, he'd used a rifle. Which might be equipped with a night scope. If so, he wouldn't have any trouble tracking them when they left the maze.

''Judas,'' Rafe muttered, still holding Anna. ''I should have known.''

''You couldn't have.'' She pulled him closer still, clinging to him.

She was wrong. The signs were all there, but he hadn't been able to stop Sheldon from coming after them to get his revenge.

''So what do we do?'' she asked.

He stared down at Anna, meeting her eyes in the darkness. There wasn't enough time to let her know all the things he felt in his heart.

Anna spoke before he could say anything. ''Just tell me what you need me to do, and I'll do it.''

It was a generous offer, one that terrified him more than anything else about this situation. He couldn't leave her in the maze in case the dogs returned. Or Sheldon. Yet, taking her with him was a huge risk as well.

Too bad he didn't have a choice.

''Come on,'' Rafe said before he could change his

mind. He took her by the arm and started running toward the mouth of the maze. "I don't want you to take any chances," he instructed. "If you hear shots, get down and stay down, understand?"

"And what about you?"

"I have to get inside the building. Since we've messed up his plans, Sheldon will probably go after Colonel Shaw and then try to double back to come after us."

They'd covered several yards before Rafe noticed Anna was limping. She had been injured, but there was no time to question her about it or curse the fact that Sheldon had hurt her. Rafe scooped her up in his arms, swung her over his shoulder and kept running.

It was like a nightmare. Running through the dark maze, wondering what would be at the end waiting for them. But Rafe had something on his side that Sheldon didn't. Sheldon's quest for revenge had driven him to this point. Rafe knew his motivation was much stronger. Anna and his baby's lives were at stake.

He stopped about twenty feet from the maze entrance and deposited her on the ground. With each step that he'd run, Rafe had tried to come up with a plan, and he thought he finally had one. Not necessarily a good one, but it might work if they got lucky.

Very lucky.

He pressed the gun into her hand and pulled back

the hedges to reveal another of the man-made slits. "Wait in here until I get back. Kill the dogs if they return."

She shook her head. "But what will you do? God, you can't go unarmed after Sheldon."

Yes, he would. He didn't have a choice. "I'll find a weapon as soon as I'm inside." Maybe. And if not, he'd go after Sheldon with his bare hands.

Rafe couldn't waste any more time so he maneuvered her into the slit, pushing back as many of the branches as he could to minimize the scratches and scrapes. He pressed a quick kiss on her mouth.

Anna caught his arm when he started to move away. "If something goes wrong—"

"It won't," Rafe interrupted.

And, damn it, it was more than an empty parting promise to help calm her. He wouldn't lose her. One way or another, he would stop Sheldon and come back for her.

"If something goes wrong," Anna repeated. "I just want you to know I love you."

I love you. Hard to hear words like that from Anna and not let them affect him.

Pushing aside her hand, he caught her by the back of the neck and kissed her. Not a brief touch of reassurance. A real kiss. One he hoped she'd remember in case it ended up being their last.

Rafe had already broken the embrace and was ready to run across the open lawn when he heard the nearly muffled shot. It was another round from that rifle, and Sheldon had fired it into the maze.

Damn it—in the maze.

Maybe he'd already finished off Shaw and had returned for Anna. After all, Sheldon certainly would have had enough time to double back, shoot Shaw, and then return to the second floor to make sure the dogs had taken care of Anna.

Rafe didn't waste any time cursing Murphy's Law. "There's been a slight change in plans. You have to come with me."

He grabbed her and ran. When they reached the entrance, he stopped to check out their surroundings and motioned for Anna to stay behind him.

There were just enough interior lights for Rafe to spot the shooter's location. A rifle was sticking out the window of the room where he'd originally left Anna.

And yes, the rifle was aimed right at the maze.

Either Sheldon had already located them with some infrared equipment, or else he would continue to fire random shots in the hopes of getting lucky. Rafe didn't care much for either scenario.

That meant he had to act fast.

The easiest way to do that was for Rafe to shoot him. It would be a tough shot, though, since he couldn't actually see Sheldon's position. And if he missed, Sheldon would know their location and would almost certainly get off some rounds. Perhaps at Anna.

However, if he kept Sheldon occupied while he got closer to the building, then Anna and he would both be safe. Well, as safe as he could make them considering there was a gunman apparently hell-bent on killing them.

From somewhere in the maze, he heard one of the dogs. A gruff snarl. Not nearby, though, so Rafe dismissed it.

Until he heard the next shot.

It went straight in the direction of that gruff snarl, and Rafe heard the dog yelp in pain. That told him exactly what he needed to know. Sheldon did indeed have some kind of night scope on the rifle, but it wasn't accurate enough to distinguish between the dogs and them.

Rafe looked at her over his shoulder. "I have to go—"

She grabbed on to him. "No!"

"Yes. Sheldon will shoot at anything that moves. Especially you. I need to do something to lead him away from the maze."

"But what about you, Rafe? You can't just make yourself a target."

He could. And would. But there was no reason to let her know that. "When you hear shots, slide through the opening and head toward the storage depot. It's nearby, not far to your left. Shut yourself in and wait.''

''No. There has to be another way. You can take me with you. Both of us can divert Sheldon.''

Rafe had already opened his mouth to tell her that wasn't going to happen, but he heard a shot. A partially silenced blast of deadly power. This one slammed into the maze. Close. Too close. Seconds later, Sheldon fired again.

And again.

Rafe scrubbed his hand over his face. Since the moment when Sheldon fired that first shot, Rafe had known all along what the most logical thing to do was. Too bad it didn't feel logical. And time was running out. Fast.

''Can you run with your foot hurt?'' he asked, taking the gun from her.

She nodded.

He hadn't thought she would say differently. Now he only prayed it was true.

''Stay behind me,'' he instructed. There was no way he could leave her in that maze with Sheldon firing a deadly barrage of bullets that might never end until he hit his ultimate target—Anna.

I love you.

Her words burned through his head as his pulse pounded in his throat. He forced himself to push her confession aside. Forced himself not to think about exactly what was at stake here.

Rafe took her through the crevice. It was their best chance at creating a blind spot for Sheldon. Still, Rafe didn't count on that. He pulled her through to the lawn and pushed her to the ground.

He waited—long agonizing seconds—to see if those bullets would come their way. Sheldon continued to fire, but it seemed random. Or else he wanted Rafe to believe it was, anyway. It was possible that the moment they moved farther into the yard, Sheldon would already have them targeted.

Keeping his gun aimed and ready, Rafe maneuvered Anna behind him and started across the yard. The nearest tree, the one he'd used earlier for cover, was mere feet from them. It seemed miles away. Each inch they had to cover would mean Anna was in danger.

"Let's move," he ordered.

She stayed behind him, and they moved in unison. One step at a time.

The shots stopped.

They were still a few feet from the tree when Rafe latched on to her arm and dove for cover. Just in time. The next shot slammed into the tree only inches from them.

So, he had his answer.

Sheldon knew exactly where they were.

But then, Rafe knew where Sheldon was as well. Now that he was no longer in that maze, he had a much better angle to put a stop to all of this. Nicholas Sheldon was going down.

Rafe crouched behind the tree and took aim. Even though he couldn't see Sheldon, he could see the position of the rifle, and he estimated Sheldon's location. Rafe aimed and double tapped the trigger, pumping two shots into the narrow opening of the window.

Silence followed.

The rifle didn't move.

From the corner of his eye, he saw a slash of motion that came from near the front of the house. A man. Rafe braced himself to fire, but it wasn't Sheldon making his way across the lawn.

It was Colonel Shaw.

"What's he doing out here?" Anna asked.

Rafe didn't have an answer for that, but it was the worst possible time for Shaw to put in an appearance. "Get down, Shaw!" he yelled.

But he didn't. Shaw lifted his hand, an act of surrender, and continued to walk across the lawn right toward them.

"Shaw!" Rafe yelled again. His instinct was to go after him, to get him away from Sheldon's aim.

But it wasn't his first instinct.

Rafe's first instinct was to protect Anna and their child. At all costs. Even if it meant violating a cardinal rule of not losing a fellow combat rescue officer.

"Sheldon?" Shaw called out. He stopped and faced the balcony. He lowered his hands and propped them on his hips, an almost cocky stance. Rafe could just make out the pistol that Shaw had tucked in the back waist of his battle-dress uniform. Not that it would do him much good. Before he could even draw his weapon, Sheldon would kill him.

"It's me that you want," Shaw continued. "You want me to pay for Eve DeCalley's death. All right, here's your chance. Just leave Rafe and Anna out of this."

Rafe didn't wait for Sheldon to respond because he figured that response would be a shower of bullets. He shoved all thoughts from his head and relied on his training. Rote skills that had been honed for situations just like this. It was combat and rescue in its purest form.

He rolled out from behind the tree, moving away from cover, and came up on one knee. His aim was automatic since he never took his eyes off the target. Rafe emptied the rest of his rounds into the space around the rifle.

Sheldon staggered forward. There was blood. But not enough. None at all in the chest area, which meant he was probably wearing a bulletproof vest. Even though Rafe had managed to wing him a couple of times in the arm, Sheldon still had the rifle clutched in his hand.

And Sheldon aimed the rifle at Shaw.

"Stay put," Rafe ordered Anna, and using the trees for cover, he started across the yard toward Shaw. He would have given just about anything for one more bullet to finish Sheldon off.

"You shouldn't have had Eve as the lead on that mission," Sheldon ground out. "She wasn't ready." He stumbled, but the windowsill stopped his fall.

Shaw was still in danger.

Sheldon took aim again. "You shouldn't have allowed her to die."

"Eve was just doing her job."

Damn it! Why was Shaw antagonizing him? He should have been trying to talk Sheldon into putting down that gun. Rafe didn't dare shout yet, but he would if he had to divert Sheldon's attention from Shaw.

"So, kill me," Shaw invited. "Go ahead."

Sheldon fired. One shot. Just as Shaw dove to the side. The bullet slammed into Shaw's right hand. His shooting hand. Rafe heard the colonel groan in pain.

As Rafe got closer, he could see both sleeves of Sheldon's shirt covered with blood. The man wouldn't last long, but he didn't need to last long to fire one final shot.

"Sheldon!" Rafe yelled.

He stepped out into what he knew was a direct line of fire. Sheldon swung the rifle toward him, just as Rafe had hoped he would.

What he hadn't counted on was hearing Anna's voice. "Sheldon!"

Rafe whipped his gaze in her direction, fearing the worst, and soon having that fear confirmed. She wasn't behind the tree but out in the open, and she was running across the side of the yard. Not toward him. But away. In an attempt to divert Sheldon's attention.

"Get back, Anna!" It took Rafe a moment to realize he hadn't shouted that, but Shaw had stolen the words from his mouth.

Rafe lurched forward into a crisscross run, praying Sheldon would focus on him.

He didn't.

As Rafe feared he would do, he turned the rifle on Anna. She was the common denominator between Shaw and Rafe. Sheldon could hurt them both by killing her.

"Rafe," Shaw called out.

It happened fast. Shaw pulled the gun from the back waist of his uniform and tossed it to Rafe. Rafe had his stance braced even before he snatched the pistol from the air.

He fired.

And fired.

Sheldon never even dropped the rifle. Still clinging to it, he toppled out of the window and fell to the ground below.

With his gun still poised to shoot, Rafe ran to Sheldon and checked to make sure he was dead.

He was.

When he turned around to tell the others, Anna was already on her way to him. They covered the distance in just a few short steps.

Rafe pulled her into his arms and held on.

"It's over?" she asked. The words were all breath, no sound. And there were already tears in her eyes.

"It's over."

Epilogue

"You're trembling," Anna whispered.

"Am I?" Rafe stroked his mouth over hers. "It's the effect you have on me. Don't mention it to Rico, though. He'll make wussy jokes about it."

From over his shoulder, Anna caught a glimpse of Cal Rico, Rafe's best man. The wink he gave her let her know that he would indeed make wussy jokes about it. It was one of the testosterone-mandated requirements of Alpha Team members. And close friends.

Rafe would no doubt enjoy every minute of the banter.

"How about you?" Rafe asked her. "Are you doing any trembling?"

"From head to toe." Anna smiled. "But it's a good kind of trembling."

"Then we must be doing the right thing." Rafe gently took her hand and slipped the wedding ring on her finger. "No turning back now, darling. You just promised to love, honor and cherish me in front of all these people.''

Anna made a passing glance of those people. All four of them. Janine, Luke Buchanan, Rico and Colonel Shaw. Even though it'd only been three days since the ordeal with O'Reilly, Quivira and Sheldon, none of them looked the worse for wear. Well, with the exception of Shaw, who had a bandage around his wounded hand.

Still, it was something of a small miracle that they'd all managed to survive and were here to share this special day with them. Everyone was safe, including their baby. They'd had test after test, and all of them confirmed that the carbon monoxide hadn't caused any damage. Those results were the answers to many prayers.

''Okay, here's the deal, darling.'' Rafe kept his voice low and intimate. The words were meant only for her. ''This might be just a simple ring, but all that forever-together symbolic stuff goes right along with it. I'm talking a permanent hip-joining of me, you and our little officer trainee that you're commissioning inside you. So, if you have any doubts—''

''I don't.''

Anna looked down at the delicately etched white-gold band. It was perfect. Like her husband. Like her healthy unborn child. Like everything else in her life. ''I guess this proves you love me. You married me twice.''

"Darling, you didn't need this ceremony to prove that. I do love you."

The words sent a warmth through her whole body. She'd never tire of hearing Rafe say that to her. "I love you, too."

The minister cleared his throat, apparently a gesture to get them to hurry things along.

They ignored him.

"I'd marry you a thousand times, Anna Mc-Quade," Rafe added. "Make that a million. And that includes any honeymoon duties expected of me." Rafe grinned and looked at the minister. "Can I kiss her now?"

"Absolutely."

Rafe slipped his arm around her waist and eased her to him. "Brace yourself. I want you to remember this for the rest of your incredibly long life."

Despite the warning, Anna didn't even try to brace herself. She wanted to surrender to whatever Rafe had in mind.

He kissed both of her cheeks first. Not basic husbandly pecks, either. Lingering caresses with that incredibly sexy, damp mouth of his.

It was just the beginning.

Rafe dipped her back. Just slightly. Just enough to throw her a little off-kilter and make the candlelight shimmer in his eyes. The jungle-hot look he gave her had Anna zinging even before his mouth came to hers.

His lips were soft and warm. Amazing. About a million steps past clever. He gave with those lips. Took in return. Satisfied. Aroused. Promised. It was pure, uncut intimacy, and like everything that Rafe McQuade did in life, it left her in awe.

He pulled back and gave her a satisfied smile.

There were no jolts. No funny feelings. And definitely no doubts. Everything was as clear as fine glass.

Anna looked into Rafe's eyes and knew she was and always would be well loved.

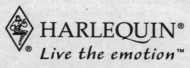